THE ACE'S BOUNTY

THE BARBER BROTHERS' FIRST ADVENTURE

JASON B. BAKER

GREER

BOOKS

THE ACE'S BOUNTY

E-BOOK ISBN-13: 979-8-9884806-0-0

PAPERBACK ISBN-13: 979-8-9884806-1-7

This novel is a work of fiction. Any references to historical events, real people, or real places are used fictitiously. Other names, characters, places, and events are products of the author's imagination, and any resemblance to actual events, places, or persons, living or dead, is entirely coincidental.

Cover Design by Book Cover Zone

Also By

"This writer has a future in the genre."

-RON SCHWAB, Bestselling author of Coldsmith, *Old Dogs, The Accidental Sheriff*, and other classic Western novels.

The Barber Brothers' Adventures

The Ace's Bounty

The War Remains

The Legacy Stand

Barber Brothers' Adventures Prequel

The Sheriff's Pursuit

The Vengeance of Reed Caine

Red Canyon Reckoning

River's Fortune

Sins of Santa Fe

Narrative Non-Fiction

Chicago To Appomattox: The 39th Illinois Infantry In The Civil War

Learn more about Jason and his books, and sign up for future updates at JasonBakerAuthor.com

To my wife, who understands the importance of writing to my life... even while honest enough to admit Civil War history and Western-style adventures aren't her thing.

And to my boys, who I hope become as close as these Barber brothers.

The purpose of life is not to be happy. It is to be useful, to be honorable, to be compassionate, to have it make some difference that you have lived and lived well.

Ralph Waldo Emerson

CONTENTS

Prologue

—•—

Pilot Knob, Missouri—September 1864

Frank Tucker sat in the chair with his hands tied tight behind him. Looking around the small tent, he frowned at its dirty sides, the humid nighttime air, and the smell. Oh, how he hated the smell. Dirty men, smoke, horses, and their waste. Many of the men regularly remarked how much they loved the smell of all the good saddle leather, but the other smells overpowered his nostrils. *Forget the fighting and dying part,* he thought. *I don't understand why anyone would put up with all of this camp life for some pointless war.*

Tucker had left home to prove everyone wrong, that his family wasn't a failure—or at least he wasn't. He had thought donning a uniform and joining the cause would lead to respect and prosperity when he returned home to Indiana. The self-righteousness he perceived from the other men rubbed him wrong, however. He did learn about himself, though. He realized he cared about himself far more than his country or fellow man. When the Union army started offering bounties to join regiments in need—payments to join specific units rather than waiting to be drafted—he saw an opportunity. He would desert, sign back up in a different regiment, receive a new bounty with a new name, then do it all over again. Along the way, he discovered that the average man was a terrible card player and that he could fill his pockets playing poker.

His sign-up and desert scheme had finally been discovered, though. This time, there had been an excellent bounty to sign up and a follow-up payment after ninety days of service. Waiting had been his downfall: having to avoid being killed in skirmishes on numerous occasions, then having the captain come to him with the accusation.

If Tucker didn't find a way out of this tent, he'd be delivered up to the provost marshal in the morning, hanged or shot, and it would all be for nothing. He had an emerging scheme back home, but it required him to get back with some extra funds. He eyed his knapsack in the corner, the original bounty, his regular pay, and the pay of other men from poker games contained within. He need only get out of this chair, grab the bag, steal a horse, and ride off. Simple enough.

"Stephens, is that you out there guarding your old friend?" That Private Stephens didn't know his real name was Frank Tucker didn't bother him one bit. He'd made sure to have one of the weak-minded ones feel they were close friends in every regiment in case he needed help. Thankfully, one of them was now his guard.

The glum-faced private stuck his head inside the tent. "Yeah, its me."

"You're just doing your job," Tucker said. "Listen, this night ain't cooling off one bit. Could I get a swallow?"

Private Stephens stepped inside and opened his canteen, holding it to Tucker's lips.

"Thanks," Tucker said. He took a long drink. "That helps make this a little less miserable. You're a good friend." He smiled broadly.

Stephens took the canteen back and looked at him, frowning. "You really done what they say?

"It ain't true," Tucker responded. He hated speaking like such an ordinary man. "They'll deliver me up tomorrow, though, and my case will win out." He looked up at the private with wide-open eyes. "Will you say a good word for me, friend?"

"I aim to," Stephens said. "You been a good friend when a lot of fellas give me a hard time." The private leaned his rifle against the edge of the tent and took a drink of water himself.

Tucker eyed the rifle, then looked at his knapsack. "Hey, Stephens, you want to see that card trick again? I'll show you how to do it. There's a deck in the top of my bag, there."

Stephens's eyes lit up, and he retrieved the cards. Returning to Tucker in the chair, the private pursed his lips. "You ain't gonna tell nobody if I untie you?"

"You can tie me right back up after I show you," he said.

Private Stephens pulled a knife from his belt and stepped behind the chair, cutting the rope and replacing the blade.

Tucker rubbed and flexed his wrists and smiled. "Let's see those cards."

He shuffled them, scanning Private Stephens, his gear, and his surroundings. Finally, he spread the cards out and told Stephens to pick one. "Alright, now don't show me. Take a look, memorize it, and put it back in."

The young private smiled, carefully selected a card, then analyzed it before placing it back in the deck.

Tucker closed up the deck, sliding his thumb in to mark it, then began shuffling, keeping track of where the card was. *I almost feel bad he can't figure this out.*

"Alright, now I'll show you after, but try to pay real close attention while I do it." He finished shuffling, and the private leaned in close, still grinning.

Tucker launched out of the chair, pinning the unsuspecting soldier to the ground. Stephens's eyes and mouth were wide open. "I'm sorry; you're a means to an end." Tucker removed the knife from the private's belt and plunged it into his chest, doing his best to muffle the howl with his hand. The rush was unlike anything he had ever felt in his life.

"What's going on in there?!" The voice was followed by the tent's flap being pulled open and a second guard entering. Tucker grabbed the rifle and swung the stock at the guard's head, knocking him to the ground, out cold.

Tucker looked back at Private Stephens, his eyes still wide, tilting his chin to look at the knife in his chest, blood coming from the corner of his mouth. Tucker gathered his knapsack and quickly rifled through Stephens's bag for foodstuffs.

Standing over the dying man, he saw him staring back, rapidly blinking. *Of course, I did it,* he thought. *Or maybe he wants to know how the trick ended?*

Tucker knelt next to the chair and picked up the dropped cards. Removing the one on top, he flipped an ace around so Stephens could see it. "Is this your card?" He dropped it on the soldier's uniformed chest. Then, he walked out of the tent, blending into the commotion on his way out of camp.

Lafayette

—•—

Eight months later . . . Lafayette, Indiana—May 1, 1865

Six men rode into town in a drizzle, the rising sun muffled by gray skies. The downtown area was off to a quiet start for a Monday morning, the whole city seemingly having been gathered at the train station at three-thirty for the important arrival.

The men passed houses and businesses adorned with flags, bunting, and black mourning badges before arriving just down the street from Merchants Bank. The lead rider was an average-sized man with a beady-eyed stare that fixed people in their place. He had black, wavy hair and was clean-shaven except for a bushy mustache and bearded chin that made his mouth entirely disappear.

He casually pulled a pocket watch from his waistcoat and held a hand up to his men. "Patience, boys." Shortly after six-thirty, just as their man had ascertained from chatting up locals earlier in the week and at the train station, the young assistant to the bank president unlocked the bank's front door and entered.

With a nod, the leader's posse began to pull flour sacks with eye and mouth holes over their heads, then dismounted their horses. The beady-eyed man casually put his pocket watch back in his waistcoat and swung down from his horse. Placing his bowler hat on his saddle and donning his flour sack, he straightened the short-fitting coat of his sack suit and followed his men to the door. Finding it had been locked again, he knocked softly.

"Um, yes?" The answer was distracted and shouted from a back office.

"Good day, friend. I'm from out of town but was hoping I could conduct a transaction."

"I'm terribly sorry, sir," came the reply, the voice moving closer to the door. "What with the president's funeral train having just come through and such, things are off to a slow start this morning." There was a fumbling of keys and the sound of a door unlocking. "If you'll come back later or tell me your name and where you're staying, I—"

With a nod of the leader's head, one of his men threw open the door, and the posse of armed men stormed into the bank, knocking the young bank assistant to the ground.

"It appears you have opened after all," the leader remarked as he strolled inside and closed the door behind him. He turned to the assistant on the floor and clapped his hands together. "Let us conduct our business then. Someone please help this gentleman to his feet."

One of the masked men helped the assistant up, and he quickly backpedaled away from the group, breathing heavily, his eyes darting around. One of the bandits covered the door while another began peering out the window. The remaining three followed their boss to the vault door as he motioned for the bank assistant to join them.

"What's your name, son?"

"Sam . . . Samuel," he managed.

"Well, Sam Samuel, here's the situation we find ourselves in. The tellers and the president still won't be in for a bit, the town is half asleep from the affairs of the morning, and we know your sheriff and city marshal are busy seeing everything is wrapped up nicely at the train station. So it's just the seven of us!" The leader gestured at the men and smiled as if Samuel were a party guest.

"What do you want, mister?"

"Ah, straight to business then." The man adopted a more unfriendly tone. "Well, Samuel, you're going to open up this vault, my men are going to fill their bags with money, and then we're just going to walk out of here, mount our horses, and ride on out.

"And if I don't?"

The leader gave a mock-disappointed frown. "Oh, Samuel, I think you know what happens then. Do you have a handful of armed associates standing ready nearby?"

Samuel shook his gravely.

"Well then, let's get that safe open," the leader said.

Samuel stepped to the vault and began opening it.

"Excellent decision. You know, Samuel, my father used to always tell me that if you did the right thing no matter what, everything would always turn out alright. He was a failure in just about everything, however—never made any money, never got any respect." He looked to see if Samuel was listening to him. "I bet you aren't supposed to open up that vault for us, or are supposed to follow some other procedure to buy time and keep us from robbing you, aren't you?"

Samuel finished opening the vault and nodded meekly.

"Think of it, though, Samuel. Surely people don't consider robbing a bank the right thing to do, and you're not doing the *right* thing, either." He paused as if to emphasize his upcoming point. "Yet I'm going to leave here a little bit richer, and you'll still be alive!"

The leader turned his attention to his burly man stationed near the door. "How are we looking?"

"Ain't nobody out there, boss."

The leader nodded, walked to a small desk and chair, and sat down as his men filled their bags. Samuel watched, bewildered, as the leader casually pulled out a deck of cards and began shuffling. "Are you a poker player, Samuel?"

Samuel shook his head.

"A shame," the man said. He dealt out a mock game before him, looking at each imaginary player's hand. "I see poker and life the same way. I have this"—he paused and twirled his hand near his head—"ability to see who I can take advantage of or who is a threat. I have taken advantage of you, Samuel, but I knew you weren't a threat."

Their bags filled, the leader stood and walked over to Samuel. "You made an excellent decision, Sam. I regret you received the short end of this transaction, but thankfully you'll live to conduct more fruitful ones going forward." Turning toward his men and gesturing toward the door, he stopped at the window. "And I see the rain has even stopped. Lovely for our ride out."

As the leader stepped into the street, he saw the city marshal arriving at his office opposite the bank. The marshal looked back at the stranger, then at the armed men exiting the bank behind him.

"What in the world is the meaning of this?" The marshal stepped into the street, and the leader did the same.

"This is regretful, Marshal," the leader said as if speaking of the rainy day. "Truly awful timing." He turned to his men and motioned to lower their weapons with his hands. Turning back to the marshal, he announced, "I'm afraid we've soured this somber day by robbing the bank."

The marshal took another step forward and watched as the men lowered their weapons. His eyes began to dart among the group.

"Are *you*, armed too?" The marshal's voice was unsteady. "Get those hands in the air."

"Why yes, I am," the leader replied. He watched the marshal gulp nervously. "So, seeing the disadvantage we have you at, Marshal, we're going to walk to our horses and leave town now."

Before the marshal could even get his rain slicker aside and put a hand on the butt of his revolver, the heist leader reached into his coat for his Colt .31-caliber Pocket Model and fired a shot into the marshal's forehead, dropping him instantly into a puddle in the street.

The leader lowered his gun and shook his head. Replacing the weapon, he took the deck of cards from a pocket and began shuffling them as he walked toward the marshal. Reaching the man's body, his men watched him kneel on the ground. "I wish you hadn't reached for that gun, Marshal."

Finding the card he was looking for, he placed an ace over the bullet wound on the marshal's forehead and returned the deck to his pocket. Rising and wiping off his knees, he nodded toward the group's horses and moved toward his own. "Off we go then."

Riding past the bank assistant now cowering in the doorway, the thief abruptly reined his horse to a stop. "I'm terribly sorry. Where are my manners? You asked my name earlier." He doffed the hat he had put back on over his flour sack. "Please just call me Ace." He gave his horse a light kick and was on his way again.

The Brothers

Rural Danville, Illinois—early June 1865

Elijah Barber finished pounding another board in place to restore what had once been a good chicken coop. Whether it or anything on the farm would ever be so again remained to be seen. He pulled off his slouch hat and ran a hand through the thick, brown hair matted to his head with sweat. He might have looked the part of a tall, muscular, and lean farmer a few years from thirty, but the mental and physical aches he had suffered were of a man twice his age.

Elijah's focus was getting a crop in for the following spring, bringing his father's farm back to life, and taking care of his younger brother, Moses. The brothers had sent back most of their pay during the war to settle up with lenders and returned with very little to their name. Upon returning, they had not got a crop in and used up what little savings they had left to scratch by through the summer before they could hire out for the fall harvest.

He looked up to see Moses finish pounding a board, then saw him nod toward the short lane leading up to their tiny cabin. Elijah turned and saw a lone rider. The old paint he recognized, but the man he did not. Moses ducked his head inside the old chicken coop and re-emerged, holding a shotgun.

"Alright, let's just see who it is," Elijah said. He watched Moses lean the gun against the coop, then cross his arms and do the same. The brothers had returned home one day to some would-be thieves who thought the farm had been abandoned, and Moses had ensured the weapon was within reach on the rare occasions they had unknown visitors.

The man was tall, in a handsome suit and fancy hat, Elijah noticed. He also saw the left arm of the man's coat was cut off and pinned at the shoulder. The rider stopped the horse a few paces from Elijah, who saw the man's eyes glance toward Moses and the shotgun.

"I realize folks are wary of strangers riding up to their property," the man said. *He has an intelligent and commanding voice*, Elijah thought to himself. "I was told to tell you that Benjamin sent me from town."

"Well, that explains the horse," Elijah said. He removed a handkerchief from his old cavalry uniform pants and wiped his brow. Benjamin was the old, half-blind livery stable owner in town that Elijah had known his whole life. Growing up where he did, he was also the only Black man he'd ever known in his entire life. As Benjamin told the story, he didn't fully recall how he had ended up in Danville but grew up working for the livery owner. When the man died, he left the business to Ben.

The man had a very formal presence and, in addition to the fine suit, a perfectly manicured dark mustache and a patch of hair on his chin. Ben having sent him made Elijah a little more at ease, but the man could have stuck a gun in his face, and Ben may not have noticed. What Elijah especially saw, however, peeking out from underneath the man's coat, was the badge on his vest. "You some kind of law, sir?"

"Indeed I am," the man answered. "Pardon my lack of introduction; my name is Solomon Foster; I'm the new U.S. Marshal for the District of Indiana."

Moses shifted his weight from the barn and laughed. "Well, mister, we're awful close, but Indiana is about seven or eight miles that way." He jerked his thumb to the east.

The marshal grinned. "Well, don't I know it. We have federal jurisdiction though, and each region has a . . ." He trailed off, apparently aware the man was fooling with him.

Elijah turned and glared at Moses, then looked back at the marshal. "I believe my brother just means to say we're a little confused, is all."

"To be understood," the marshal replied. "I'd be happy to explain myself. The livery owner, uh, Benjamin, said I should talk to an Elijah Barber."

"Well, Marshal, you found him," Elijah replied. "That geography expert there is my younger brother, Moses."

Moses tipped a finger to the brim of his straw hat and replaced the shotgun inside the chicken coop. "Can't imagine puttin' holes in a marshal with the scatter gun would go very well."

"Marshal, I don't reckon I know what we can do for you, but we been workin' all morning, and it was time to eat anyhow." He looked up to the bright sun to confirm his belief. "You're welcome to join us."

The marshal swung down from the horse more adeptly than Elijah would have guessed with the missing arm and straightened his suit coat. "Well, I'd be much obliged, Mr. Barber."

MARSHAL FOSTER FOLLOWED Elijah and Moses into the small cabin and sat at the homemade wooden table when Elijah offered a chair. The place was primitive but well-kept—a fireplace with a large, sturdy kettle, a table, and two rocking chairs. A small bed was in one corner and a cot in the other. A large army-issue trunk sat next to each sleeping position.

"Just the two of you?" The marshal accepted some water with a nod. "I hate to pry but saw the two gravestones in the yard."

"Our parents," Elijah offered as he sat down with some water himself. "Pa died in fifty. Just dropped in a field one day. Our mother died the fall after the war started." Elijah never talked about this to most people. While maintaining his composure, he struggled mightily with failing to support the family when his father died and caring for his brother when his mother passed.

The marshal gulped down the cold well water. "Well, I'm awfully sorry to hear that. You have my condolences."

Elijah nodded, and Moses joined them at the table, setting down a plate of biscuits and a bowl of beans. He put a plate in front of each man, then, almost as an afterthought, reached into a nearly bare cupboard and dug out a spoon formed from a gourd for the bowl of beans.

Moses sat down, bowed his head, and began to pray, but Elijah cut him off, hoping to get the measure of his guest. "Marshal Foster, normally Moses here does the prayin', but I'd like to give the honor to our guest, if you'd be so kind."

"Be happy to," the marshal said. He bowed his head. "Lord, I thank you for the kindness of strangers and making new friends. Bless this humbly shared meal, and bless these Barber boys. Amen."

"Amen," echoed the brothers. Moses dug in, and Elijah admired the lawman who had offered such an appropriate grace. Elijah didn't consider himself overly pious, but they'd been raised as a church family. He and Moses had just kept praying before meals as something familiar to do. He watched the marshal ladle some beans onto his plate, then did the same and grabbed a biscuit.

The marshal also reached for a biscuit and made a face when he realized how hard it was.

Moses noticed and spoke up. "Sorry 'bout that, Marshal. But if you sop it around in those beans it'll work out alright."

Elijah felt a deep twinge of embarrassment at the only meal they could offer the man.

The marshal smiled and nodded. "I'm sure it will, and thank you for preparing it." He split the biscuit in half and set each side on the beans.

"Not to be rude then, Marshal," Elijah said, "but what it is then that we can do for you?"

"Yes," said the marshal, wiping his mouth with his hand. "Not that I don't appreciate a nourishing meal, but I did not ride in from Danville just for this." He gave an apologetic look to Moses, who only raised his hands in surrender and then resumed eating.

"Yeah, what does bring the good marshal of the Indiana district to our neck of the woods," asked Moses with a mouthful of food.

Elijah gave Moses the same look he had outside and noticed the marshal caught him doing so. *Why does he always have to act so clever?* Elijah thought to himself. He glared at his brother for another moment. They were opposites beyond their attitudes as well. Moses wasn't as tall as Elijah but was more muscular. He had thin red hair but a full beard. Elijah sometimes thought that Moses grew the beard just to be different from him.

"Well, gentlemen," the marshal said, pushing his plate away, "I believe you two can be of great help to me."

Elijah stared at the man intently while Moses laughed. They were all quiet for a moment before Elijah spoke up. "Marshal, unless you're paying good money for help with harvest this fall, I'm not sure what help we can be to you."

The brothers looked at the marshal with curious eyes, and he returned the gesture.

"You boys served in the war, yes?" He asked the question matter of factly, then sat back.

Moses looked at Elijah for approval. He gave a slight nod. There had been scant word about the war since returning to their empty farm.

"Independent cavalry company attached to an infantry regiment made up mostly of fellas from town," Moses said. "Elijah was our captain there, and I"—he paused—"was a sergeant. The farm was all but a total failure by what should have been harvest time, so when Ma died, we joined up. We figured we didn't know how to run a farm but could shoot and ride."

The talk of being off to war and dead parents hung in the air momentarily as the table fell silent. Then Marshal Foster turned to Elijah and spoke up. "So, you were a company commander?"

"They needed farm boys to round out the company. Captain initially went to a businessman's son from in town, but they made me a second lieutenant for bringing in the farm boys. Got sent to Cairo on garrison duty, then the same near Fort Davidson in Missouri. Our three years were up in January, and we came back home to . . ." He paused and looked out the window. "Well, not to get any crops in; that's for sure."

The marshal finished a bite of his biscuit and asked, "No action, then?"

"Not for a while, but then . . ."

The marshal nodded gravely. "They made you captain when yours were killed then?"

Elijah's eyes sparked with recognition. "That's right. You served, Marshal?"

Marshal Foster looked down where his missing arm would have been and then back at Elijah. "I was a full colonel leading a regiment with Grant moving down the Mississippi. Helluva thing to see that man operate up close knowing what he turned into out east." He paused for the effect of knowing the general the brothers were no doubt aware of. "Lost the arm during the Vicksburg campaign, and they sent me to Cairo to do some staff and logistics work. Put a star on while I was there."

"A general! At our table!" Moses smiled and tipped a biscuit to his head in salute.

"Only briefly, son, and not in the field at that."

Elijah shifted uncomfortably in his seat. "I'm still unclear why you're here, then."

"Well, my wife's kin is originally from St. Louis, and she spent the war years there. I spent my whole life in Indiana and finished law school just before the war started. I left Cairo when the fighting ended and made my way to St. Louis for a job in a law office with my father-in-law. When Johnson became president, there was some moving around of judicial appointments and such, and I got asked if I wanted to be a marshal back home."

The brothers looked at him expectantly.

"I'll be straight with you boys. My father-in-law is a connected man, and I'd like to be a judge or politician maybe, someday. Adding some lawman work to the war and lawyer resume doesn't hurt none, especially in my home state."

Elijah sensed the man's embarrassment at the patronage but appreciated his honesty.

"Listen, fellas," the marshal continued. "I may have gotten this through political dealings, but I believe in the work and think I'm qualified to do it. I went to law school 'cause I believe in justice and fought in the war because I believe in this Union of ours." He tapped the silver star on his chest and continued.

"I left St. Louis a couple of days ago on a train bound for Lafayette, where they've just had some trouble. I stopped in Danville to see a friend and former marshal for advice. Renting a horse at the livery, Benjamin heard me talking about all that and how I knew I'd need some help, what with the arm and all. He suggested some close-at-hand farm boys who fought on horseback for the Union blue. Said they worked hard, needed money, and were considering getting out of town for a fresh start anyway."

Elijah pushed back from the table and looked at the ceiling as Moses clapped his hands loudly and let out a yell. "You want us to ride along as deputy marshals, don'tcha, Marshal?"

Marshal Solomon Foster looked at Elijah, knowing he was the one to convince. "That's exactly what I want, gentlemen."

The Marshal

"Real life deputy marshals; you hear that, Eli?" Moses was on his feet, moving around with an excited look. He began to settle when he looked at his older brother, however.

"Marshal, we are not lawmen. Sure, we did some fighting in the war, but we're just two farmers trying to get our land back up and running. We ain't got time for runnin' 'round serving papers when we're goin' to have to hire out for two or three busy seasons before we run our own farm again."

Moses stopped his pacing and fixed a mean stare on Elijah. Elijah glared back at him and knew he didn't have long before Moses would have something witty to say.

"You think getting this farm back to even scratching out an existence will be hard work?" Elijah asked. "Imagine if we go ridin' around Indiana and who knows where else and let things sit even longer."

"You said yourself, Eli, we might best just get out of here and find a better situation."

The marshal turned away from Elijah and toward Moses. "If your brother doesn't want to—"

"Marshal," Elijah interrupted, "if you'd take a man who'd leave his only remaining kin to fend for himself savin' their daddy's farm, then I feel even more confident in my decision." He set his stare on his brother. "Moses, get back to that chicken coop, and I'll join you after I see our guest out."

Moses began to interject but saw his brother would be unmoved and a look of resignation on the marshal's face. He grabbed his straw hat off a chair back, planted it on his head, and stormed out of the house.

"Well, Captain Barber, I suppose I had better—"

"We're somehow the only people who can help you? Couple of farmers the livery owner told you about?" He looked at the marshal expectantly as he pulled out a homemade clay pipe and filled it with tobacco.

Marshal Foster laid his hand on the table in front of him. "It is undoubtedly not the best idea, is it? However, deputies come and go as the marshals do, and that's what has happened this time. A lot of good ones were lost to the war." The marshal lowered his eyes. "*In* the war, too."

Elijah removed a match from the pipe's bowl and shook it out. "I understand your predicament, Marshal, I do. As I said, we ain't lawmen, though." He puffed on the pipe. "Big difference between riding at the enemy and shooting, and doing law work."

"Maybe. Maybe not," Marshal Foster said. "I hope to God not, but I bet I'll need the riding and shooting part at one point or another, though." He shifted entirely toward Elijah. "Plus, your time chasing vigilantes around the backwoods is not far from the kind of work I'll often be called on to do."

Elijah stared at the man for a moment. "I've had enough of that."

"Fair enough, Elijah." The marshal took a deep breath and relaxed into the chair. "If I can just finish my pitch, however, and know I did all I could. You'd each make twenty-five percent of what I earn. I get two hundred dollars a year, paid out monthly whenever possible.

Two dollars for serving paper, four dollars for making an arrest, and a few cents a mile for traveling to and from such affairs. Now I'm only obligated to pay you the twenty-five percent on the fees and such, but I'm not in this for the money, and I need all the help I can get."

Elijah sat back and considered this, puffing on the pipe as he heard the hammering begin on the chicken coop outside. He wanted nothing more than to do right by his father's memory and get their farm back to what it once was. He'd had a successful operation and was well respected in town for providing folks with things they needed in addition to providing for his family. He also saw how unhappy his brother was and how they'd returned from a life of having a real purpose to one of current near-poverty. His thoughts were interrupted as Marshal Foster continued.

"Now Elijah, I can appeal to your sense to be a continued part of serving the country, bringing justice, and finding some adventure in life. I think what you really want, though, is to take care of your brother and earn an honest living. This work will pay *at least* double what you boys would make hiring out, and then you'd still have to worry about if you could make the farm go again."

The marshal has a point, Elijah thought as he drummed his fingers on the wooden table and savored the smell of the tobacco. They could hire out for the harvest, sell wood over the winter, and still might not have what they need to get the farm running again.

"Plus," the marshal added, sensing he was winning Elijah over, "while we can't collect any federal reward money, this bank in Lafayette I'm about to go see has a twenty-five hundred dollar reward out for anything leading to the capture of whoever robbed them. And if he's the same man who hit some places in nearby towns, that reward might be even larger."

"And you know who it is?" Elijah asked.

"I don't," Marshal Foster admitted.

Elijah frowned.

"Well, Elijah, I've taken enough of your time." The marshal stood and offered his hand, and Elijah stood and accepted it. "I thank you for the meal and hearing me out." He pulled a pocket watch from his coat, kept on the left to reach it with his good arm, and checked the time. "I'll be staying at the inn for the evening. If you change your mind before morning, that's where I'll be."

Elijah nodded, noticing the man kept his revolver on his left, handle out, wondering how quickly he could cross-draw and fire. He walked his guest to the doorway, stopping when the marshal spun back to him suddenly.

"You know," the marshal said, pointing his finger and resting it on his chin, "if I could have the honor of your company once more in the morning, I'd love to return your hospitality and buy you breakfast. I know it's a small journey into town if you have no business there."

Moses had stopped hammering and listened to the men who had stepped outside. "C'mon now, Eli," he shouted out. "You said we needed to sell some things, and I can only do beans and biscuits so many times."

Marshal Foster chuckled. "What do you say, Elijah? I'm told the tavern puts on a nice enough morning meal."

Elijah took a long puff on the pipe, glared at Moses, and then looked back at the marshal. "We got a lot of work to do, Marshal Foster. I enjoyed your company but am sorry you came all the way out here for nothing."

Marshal Foster frowned and looked at Moses, who did the same. Putting a smile on his face, the marshal turned back to Elijah and offered his hand. "Pleasure to meet a fellow soldier, Mr. Barber."

Elijah accepted his hand and shook it, then watched the man climb into his saddle. As he rode off, Elijah tapped out the bowl of his pipe and stuck it in his back pocket as he returned to the chicken coop. He began hammering boards once again, ignoring Moses glaring at him.

Danville

The dream was always the same. The bugle was blowing; his men were running around frantically. Shouts of "He's gone" and "He's dead." Elijah was always watching himself in the dream, never seeing it through his own eyes. Watching himself storm out of his tent in the dark, fumbling around to see and asking *who* was gone and *who* was dead.

Then he would see himself looking into the prisoner's tent. There, he wouldn't see a prisoner but the bloody body of Private Stephens. Then there was Corporal Jones, trying to explain what happened to Elijah while a field surgeon did his best to sew up the gash in the side of his head.

The dream always ended the same, too. With Elijah calling out for Moses. *What happened? What happened, Mo?*

"What happened, Mo?" Elijah called out, bolting upright in bed. He took a deep breath and rubbed his eyes. The earliest bit of morning light filtered through the cabin's lone window. "Sorry if I woke you up again, Moses."

Swinging his feet out of bed, he saw that Moses wasn't on his cot. He looked over to the table and didn't see him there either. He pulled on his clothes and stepped outside, hoping to find him out there.

Trudging across the small yard, he stuck his head into the stalls in the back of the lean-to and saw Moses's sorrel was gone. *Dang it, Mo.*

ELIJAH RODE WEST toward town atop his dappled buckskin, his old mule walking free rein and pulling their farm wagon behind him. If he was headed into town, he might as well try to get a few small things of value sold. Following the county's namesake river, the Vermillion, on his left, he trekked into Danville on the same path he vaguely remembered the Potawatomi being forced through town on their way from Indiana to a Kansas reservation when he was very young. His father had told him it was an unfortunate part of progress. Then years later, Elijah fought in a war primarily over slavery and saw the violent result in a border state like Missouri up close. *Progress sure comes slowly,* he thought to himself.

The town had been a settlement of scarcely five hundred at that time. Still, Elijah and Moses saw the town's transformation over the years into one often visited by Abraham Lincoln when he rode the circuit, developing into an important coal mining area, turning into a city pushing past four thousand people. Now Elijah rode into that town alone, searching for his brother among them.

Arriving in town, Elijah walked his horse into Danville's livery stable after selling their modest produce and older tools at shops in town. Peering down the long center aisle between the stalls, Elijah called out, "Benjamin, you here?"

Elijah saw one of the boys that helped Benjamin poke his head around a corner with a smile and point into a stall at the end of the row.

"Ol' Ben, you in here?" Elijah asked. He shook his head at the man's hearing, which was now apparently as bad as his vision.

"Who's that now?"

Elijah heard a shuffling in the stall, then saw the eighty-year-old man amble into the aisle and begin squinting in his direction.

"Benjamin, it's Elijah."

"Well, I'll be," he said weakly. "Elijah Barber come to see me." He strode up close to Elijah and stuck out a hand, placing the other on top after Elijah accepted it. "How them horses treatin' you boys?" Ben stroked the neck of the buckskin standing next to Elijah. The horse shook its neck and snorted in recognition.

Ben had come into possession of a pair of fine Morgan geldings and sold them to the brothers for next to nothing after hearing them reminisce about their mounts in the war. Moses chose the sorrel to match his hair and named it Copper, which was okay with Elijah, as he had taken a shine to the buckskin. He called him Bear after Moses remarked that the horse's dapple up front gave him more black than most buckskins.

"Ben, we don't have a lot to our names since we been back," Elijah said graciously, "but we got us some fine horses, thanks to you." Elijah looked around and didn't see Copper. He figured he'd find him tied to a hitching point before the tavern.

The old man had more white hair in his ears than on his head but could always hear just fine when getting a compliment, it seemed. With mock humility, he threw his hands up at Elijah. "After all your pap did for me and all you boys went through in the war . . . What you did for people look like me . . . sellin' a few good horses for cheap is no skin off my old back. What about that blind john mule?"

"Wondered if you might want him back," Elijah said. He rubbed at the back of his neck, and there was a tinge of regret. "We'd maybe rent him out in the busy season if we needed him, but . . ." Elijah trailed off, eager to avoid the embarrassment. "Can only feed so many mouths, you know."

Benjamin held up a hand, as if to say, no more. "Somebody always needs a mule, no matter how old or blind." He chuckled, and Elijah did, too.

"We met the one-armed friend you sent to our place yesterday," Elijah said.

"How's that?"

"The U.S. Marshal that you sent to recruit us," Elijah replied.

"Marshal?" Benjamin scrunched his nose. "I don't know anythin' of this one-armed business, but some feller come in here sayin' he was just stoppin' through and needed a horse for the day. Started tellin' me all these stories. Nicest guy, he was, and when he says he was in the war, I said, by God, you should go tell this to Elijah Barber and his brother."

Elijah looked at him with wide eyes. "Ben, you mean to tell me you didn't see that man had a badge on his chest and was missin' an arm?"

Benjamin pursed his lips and shook his head.

Elijah shook his head. "Says he's goin' after some bank robber in Lafayette over in Indiana."

The old man whistled a unique sound from a mouth with few teeth. "Can't say as I know it, but then I ain't been anywhere but here for goin' on pert near thirty-five years now."

"And we're all the better for it, Ben," Elijah said. He patted the man on the back. "I'll bring that mule around. Can I leave the buckskin here for an hour maybe?"

"Oh, sure. We got space and hay alike. How about that sorrel of your brother's?"

"I'm about to go look into that," Elijah said.

ELIJAH WALKED OVER to the Jenkins Inn and Tavern on Main Street. Arriving out front, he saw Moses's horse tied to the hitching post. *So much for hoping he just left to blow off some steam.* Elijah noticed there was no bedroll, and his saddlebag wasn't packed. The horse recognized him and bobbed his head. "Well, you weren't leaving for good just yet, were you, Copper?" The sorrel bobbed his head as if in agreement. Elijah patted the horse on the neck and walked up the steps.

Stepping inside, he saw the innkeeper, Ms. Jenkins, and tipped his hat before removing it. Elijah saw her daughter, Sarah, come around the corner. She was Moses's age, and he fancied her, but she had always taken a shine to Elijah.

"Well, I'll be. If it isn't Mr. Elijah Barber, right here in town. How are you, Eli?" She smiled at him broadly.

"I'm doin' just fine, Sarah; thank you for asking." He returned her smile but was scanning the tables.

"I was surprised to see Moses come in without you. Didn't figure either of you made trips into town without the other." She noticed him looking around and pointed him out.

"We don't." He saw Marshal Foster and Moses, but their backs were turned to him. "I, uh . . ." He trailed off. "It's not important."

She forced a smile and pulled Elijah aside a step. "How are you doing, really, Eli?"

"Oh, I'm alright," he started, then saw the look of concern on her face. "Why do you ask me again? And like that?"

"Well, I just mean, with being back in town and everything that happened." She smoothed her dress and looked around a bit. "It's just a bit of a mixed reception by folks in town, wouldn't you say? I don't believe they're right, but an awful lot of folks seem to blame you two for all those boys who got killed."

He looked around and saw some knowing glares from the few locals at the tables but then thought of the reception of some others and folks like Benjamin.

"They weren't there, and explaining myself likely just makes it worse," Elijah said. "I'll be alright."

She smiled and patted his arm, then turned back toward Moses. "They already ate, but you want me to bring you something? Or send out some coffee?"

"Coffee would be great," he said. He caught Moses's eye and glared at him. "Don't reckon I'll be here long enough to eat."

She gave him a pained smile and headed for the kitchen, gesturing for him to join their table as she left.

"Sarah," he called after her. "Who is that he's with?"

"The one with the badge?" Sarah raised her eyebrows. "Or the other one?"

"Believe it or not, I know the one with the badge," he said. "Do you know who the other one is?" He craned to get a look at the second man. He wore a nice suit and waistcoat and was confident-looking, with combed-back hair down to his neck and a neat mustache and beard.

"I haven't the slightest idea," she said. She disappeared toward the kitchen.

Elijah looked back at her for a moment. *Are there really that many people in town who blame me for what happened?* He shook the thought from his head as he arrived at the table.

"Ah, Elijah," Marshal Foster said. He and the unknown man stood while Moses dropped his fork and hung his head. Elijah shook Marshal

Foster's hand, then turned to the other man as the marshal introduced him. "Elijah, this is Ward Hill Lamon, a former U.S. Marshal for the District of Columbia. Mr. Lamon, may I present Moses's older brother, Elijah."

"Pleased to make your acquaintance, sir," Lamon said. He shook Elijah's hand and gestured at an empty chair.

"Yes, thank you," Elijah said. He hated the routine of formal introductions, especially among accomplished people. He had barely been exposed to such things as an army captain in Missouri's backwoods. He looked down at his clothes and felt even more awkward.

Seemingly sensing Elijah's discomfort, Marshal Foster spoke up. "I'm sorry, but we already ate. Moses said you wouldn't be joining us."

"I gathered that," Elijah said curtly. He glanced at his brother and then said to Marshal Foster with a softer tone, "It's quite alright. I asked them to bring me some coffee, but I don't intend to stay long." He emphasized the last word while returning his stare to Moses. Angry but not wanting to cause an outright scene, he accepted the chair Lamon was still gesturing to.

Elijah's coffee came, and he looked closer at Moses. Elijah at least had not known he'd be attending this meeting, but Moses had made no effort to look more presentable. They were a disheveled-looking pair, attired in a mix of old uniform items and homespun clothes, wearing what were probably the finest items they owned—their army-provided, tall, black cavalry boots.

Despite his unease and anger at Moses, he attempted to be cordial. "Mr. Lamon," Elijah said, trying to sound dignified in conversation, "I assume you are the man Marshal Foster tells us used to live here in Danville for a spell?"

"I did indeed," Lamon answered. He set down his coffee. "Moved from Virginia when I was nineteen and then returned for a spell after law school. Was the prosecutor for the old eighth judicial district for a bit. That's how I came to know President Lincoln. He was riding the circuit at the time."

"No foolin'?" Moses practically spit crumbs of his breakfast out in his excitement.

Elijah cringed at his brother's demeanor. Manners weren't part of whatever plan he was concocting. "And that association led to you being a U.S. Marshal later on?" Elijah asked.

"Well, that and helping save his life," Lamon said matter-of-factly. "I helped him get his political career running here in the area and then became a bodyguard of sorts. I worked with Allan Pinkerton himself to get him safely through Baltimore on his way to be inaugurated."

Elijah gave a blank stare, and Lamon looked at each brother.

"He a friend of the president, too?" Moses continued devouring his breakfast.

If Lamon were the one doing the hiring, I wouldn't have to worry about this, Elijah thought.

"The Pinkerton Detective Agency," said Lamon, in seeming disbelief. He went on to detail the life of Allan Pinkerton, his work spying for the Union army during the war and his ever-expanding national detective agency footprint.

Moses sat back, took a big drink of coffee, and wiped his mouth. "Sounds real exciting, that does." As if Lamon had just made up a story to entertain the group.

Shifting uncomfortably at the interaction, Marshal Foster decided a reference to excitement was a good enough transition to his reason for the meeting.

"Gentlemen, I wrote to Mr. Lamon here when I was first apprised of my new job, and it just so happened he would be here visiting family when I traveled through. He has been kind enough to share his thoughts on the job with me, given his experience."

Elijah spoke up. "Marshal Foster"—he nodded to Lamon—"and Mr. Lamon. I don't mean to be impolite, but I just don't think we are the men you are looking for. And frankly, I've made that pretty clear."

"You served in the cavalry, Mr. Barber. You and your brother served your country. Now Solomon says you've returned home to a failing farm. You have no work, no prospects."

Elijah looked at the marshal, trying to remain calm.

Moses chose a different tactic. "Listen here, Mr. Lamon. I know you and the marshal got fancy law degrees and suits and you know all the right people, but my brother and I are good, hard-working, honest men. We might a' failed at farming and ain't got skills for making or fixin' things, but just because our only skills are riding and shooting don't make us lesser folks." He took a drink of coffee, then threw in an afterthought. "And that's true of my brother, whether he wants to do this or not."

Elijah spent most of his time attempting to hold off such outbursts from Moses, but he was happy for this one. He saw Moses look at him out of the corner of his eye and decided to soften his glare.

Lamon slapped the table. "Precisely gentlemen. This is why Solomon needs you as his deputies. You used your skills to hold this nation together, now use them to keep law and order. A man should be so lucky to be paid for honest work using his God-given abilities."

The marshal looked at the two brothers expectantly, and Moses did the same to Elijah. He had to admit the argument was convincing, but the unknowns still worried him.

Intuitively, Lamon jumped back into the conversation with vigor. "This thief, this bank robber in Indiana. He has defiled the name of our late president, bringing his misdeeds to the line of the funeral procession. What else was it you said was in the wire, Solomon? About his perverse actions after he has killed men?"

The marshal raised his eyebrows. "Ah, yes. I hadn't yet mentioned that to them. Apparently, the word out of Lafayette, confirmed from a storekeeper in a robbery previous, is that he carries around a deck of playing cards and places one on the wounds of the deceased."

Moses stopped eating and stared at the marshal; Elijah raised his eyebrows, looking like he had seen a ghost. His shaking hand knocked some items around on the table, causing a minor disturbance to those seated nearby.

"Just crass," Lamon said. "As if robbing and killing a man is a parlor game."

"Elijah, even if I can't talk you into it, Moses would be a great—"

"Excuse me, Marshal," Elijah interjected. He stood abruptly, the rub of the chair on the wooden floor and the sound of his voice quieting those around them. "I'd like to talk to my brother outside."

"Alright then," Marshal Foster said. He nodded at Moses, then shrugged at Lamon.

"Excuse us," Elijah said. Moses stood and reluctantly followed, giving sheepish nods to those watching.

Stepping outside onto the small porch of the tavern, Elijah pulled his slouch hat on his head and stepped off to the side, Moses joining him.

"Eli, I can explain—"

"Dang it, Mo." Elijah took his hat right back off and beat it against his leg, dust hopping off it. "Ya just leave 'fore I even wake up; make me come in here lookin' like a fool."

"I just wanted—"

"Plus, you're sittin' over there shoveling food into your mouth, ignoring even the very little bit we know about social graces. What is goin' through your mind, Moses?"

"Maybe I'm just hungry." He said it loud enough that some passers-by looked up at the brothers. They both tipped their hats and smiled.

Elijah lowered his eyes and turned his head to the side. All he cared about was taking care of the last family he had left, and here he was chewing him out for acting rash when he might have just wanted a meal.

Moses waited until Elijah looked at him again and said in a lower voice, "That farm ain't gonna happen again, Eli, and I don't rightly think either of us cares other than we need a way to get by." He rubbed his neck and looked around. "We just gonna stick to this 'cause it's all we ever known?"

"Let's head back home." Elijah smiled at one of the farm lenders they knew walking to his office. He hated keeping up appearances. The Barber brothers returned from the war to bring their daddy's farm back to life. Permanent and upstanding residents of Danville. *Ain't hardly a dollar to our name.* He wanted to wish it all away, ride home, pretend they'd never argued, and move on, like their father would have done.

"No, Eli. Tell me why we shouldn't just sell pert near everything we got, go with that marshal, and see where it takes us."

"What, Mo? Go catch a bank robber? Ride around Indiana's small towns and farmland and God knows where else chasin' a bank robber?"

"Like we ain't never done such a thing not more than nine months ago. Or we could stay here and see if we starve before getting the farm running again. Or I'm sure they'd take us at the coal mine. It ain't taking a steamer up the Missouri and hitting the western frontier like we've said, but it'd be a new start."

"Mo, men barely scratching out a living don't launch themselves into the unknown. Didn't you hear all those older fellas in the regiment talking about losing their hats heading out west to find gold? They were glad a war started and gave them a paying job."

"Exactly!" Moses threw up his hands. "Something came up they were good at, and they made a living. We learned a new skill that we can use!"

"Half of 'em is dead, Mo." Elijah took a step and pointed a finger in Moses's face. A few people stopped and stared at the scene. Elijah backed away and raised a reassuring hand. He didn't know where that last outburst had come from. Was he trying to keep Moses from dying or avoid seeing more death than he already had? Elijah turned away and leaned his arms on the porch railing. "Did you not hear me say no yesterday?"

"Do *you* not hear *me* saying I don't want to stay here and die poor and hungry and without finding any more meaning? Not when we have an opportunity, no sir." Moses looked at him and, getting no answer, continued. "Did you not hear him mention the playing card on the body? And it's a feller from Indiana, likely? You know some a' them late war bounty collectors we got were Indiana boys." Moses glared at him momentarily, then leaned down on the railing beside him. "I saw your reaction when he said it." Moses scratched his chin and let out a deep breath.

The two watched people going to and fro on the street for a moment before Moses spoke again. "Like it or not, Eli, that stuff we done in the war—what this Marshal wants us to do now—it's what we're good at."

"Don't I know it," Elijah said calmly. "And here I'd already resigned myself to comin' with to keep your rear end safe . . ." He trailed off momentarily, then turned, leaning against the railing and looking into the tavern. "Then he goes and brings up that fool playing card." He shook his head as if doing so would make this all disappear. "Mo, if I lose you . . ." He was no good at this at all. "It's worse than just failing Ma and Pa. I ain't got anythin' else."

Moses stood and looked down at Elijah, still leaning on the porch. He rested an arm on his brother's shoulder. "You think that ain't the same for me?" He smiled at his brother, then looked inside through the window, eyeing the marshal talking to Lamon. "You gotta ask him, Eli."

Elijah stood and took a deep breath. "Yeah, I know I gotta ask him." He punched Moses in the arm as he walked past. "If you were so doggone hungry, we coulda gone hunting."

The brothers returned inside, ignoring the looks of those that had witnessed their quarrel, and Elijah marched right up to Marshal Foster. "Was it an ace?"

"Pardon?"

"The card. The card the bank robber left on the body," Elijah said impatiently. "Was it an ace?

Marshal Foster's eyes shot wide open. "Yes, yes it was. How on earth would you know that?"

Moses let out a laugh and stuck his thumbs in his braces.

"Perhaps Moses and I could be of more help than I previously thought."

First Goodbye

Returning home in the afternoon, the brothers began packing up what little they had in preparation for leaving. They had primarily ridden in silence. Elijah figured they both had said their piece and that, as usual, they would carry on as the argument had never happened and would emerge again soon enough.

"Awful nice of the marshal to buy us some suits," Moses said, admiring his new clothes. They now wore dark coats and vests, new white shirts, and new pants. Moses had gotten a new wide-brimmed felt hat, but Elijah had stuck with his cavalry slouch hat. Moses packed a clean shirt and pants in a saddle bag. "Sure didn't expect such a thing."

"Well," said Elijah, opening the trunk by his bed, "I reckon he was not expecting we didn't need us some weapons." He pulled out his Colt Army Model 1860 revolver, tested the hammer, and clicked through the chamber before loading .44-caliber paper cartridges. "Apparently, he didn't"—Elijah stopped and scratched his chin while looking up at Moses—"take home any souvenirs after his service."

Moses raised his eyebrows and smiled as he removed a lever-action Spencer repeating carbine from his trunk while watching his brother do the same. He found two boxes of .56-56 cartridge tubes for the

Spencer. "Not sure we were 'sposed to, but an honest mistake after years of service."

Elijah smiled and shook his head, holstered the revolver while packing another, carrying the carbine and his bags out to Bear. Securing his saddlebags and tying a bedroll in the back, he slid the carbine into the saddle's scabbard and watched Moses complete the process himself with Copper.

Laying his arms across his horse, Elijah asked, "You ready? Said he wants to leave before sundown."

Moses looked back at the house, now empty save for their sparse furniture and the bare trunks, and turned back to Elijah. "You really think this could be the bounty jumper from Pilot Knob? I mean, what are the odds, Eli?"

"You sayin' you don't wanna go?"

Moses held up his hands in surrender. "Oh, I'm in either way."

Elijah started to move to mount his horse, then stopped and looked back to Moses. "We ought to go say goodbye."

Moses's eyes lit with realization, and he began following Elijah to the gravestones. They arrived at the rough, homemade markers with names and dates crudely chiseled.

"Haven't said hello in a while," Moses said.

"Me, either." Elijah looked up at the sky. "In fact, I guess I never really said anything to them at all out here."

"I ain't good at this," Moses said. He removed his hat and kicked at the dirt.

"Well, I ain't, neither." Elijah removed his hat as well. When Moses was silent, he assumed this would fall to the older brother. "We wanted to make this farm work for you, Pa . . ." Elijah was attempting to sound brave but trailed off. "We kept Ma fed and clothed until she went to be with you. You were right that we spent too much time ridin' around, hunting and shooting instead of learning more about the farm work."

"We learned that part well, though," Moses said.

Elijah nodded. Individually and collectively, the brothers had failed at many things, but riding and shooting were not two of them.

"We did what we could in the war. Ma, I'm not sure what all you saw up there . . ." He trailed off again, realizing she either already knew or this was pointless. "We took care of each other and fought for a worthy cause."

"And now we're gonna do that again." Moses hadn't phrased it as a question, but a glance to the side made Elijah realize it was one.

"You both wanted me to take care of Mo, 'n that's what I aim to do. We'll make a living while we're at it and see if we can't find our purpose out there." Elijah wasn't sure what else to say, so he put his hat back on his head and returned to their horses with Moses following.

They were silent momentarily, looking at each other, their arms laying across their saddles. Elijah felt there was something more to be said to his brother and sensed Moses thought the same. He wanted to apologize for chastising him but didn't want it to seem like he thought he was in the wrong. He could be sorry for getting after him, but he knew he'd deserved it. As was his custom, however, he decided not to and mounted Bear.

Moses shook his head and mounted Copper, and the two rode to the tree line and the trail that would lead them toward the road to town.

"Gonna stop and talk to him?" Moses looked at Elijah and then back at the path.

"Figure we better," Elijah said as he continued staring at the back of Bear's bobbing head. "Told the marshal I might be able to bring another."

Moses whistled and cocked his head to the side but said nothing. "This'll be something." The two brothers rode silently for a long while before seeing a small clearing in the trees and a modest cabin up a slight rise from the stream. Splashing across the shallow water, they approached the home.

As Elijah was about to call out, he heard a twig break to his right, then the unmistakable sound of a hammer being cocked. "That's close enough, boys," came the voice, whose owner emerged from behind a tree leveling a double barrel shotgun at Elijah and Moses.

"WELL GOOD LORD, Sheriff Jones," Moses cried out with a nervous laugh. "This how you go greetin' neighbors who come call on ya?"

Elijah took his hand away from the revolver he had barely gotten a hand to before seeing the shotgun. He hadn't realized he was holding his breath until he saw that it was the former sheriff, Talbot Jones.

Talbot lowered the shotgun and looked at each brother before responding to Moses. "Well, I don't get many visitors these days," he grumbled in a low, gravelly voice. "Especially not ones in fancy suits and armed to the teeth."

"I guess not," chuckled Moses, returning his revolver to its holster.

Elijah looked over his shoulder at him, then turned back to Talbot. "How are you, Sheriff? We come to ask your help on something."

"I'm fine, boys." He began walking toward the house and talking over his shoulder as the brothers followed. "Ain't the sheriff no more, neither, so we can drop that."

Elijah watched the short, barrel-chested man move and noticed his age was showing. He figured he was around sixty, the same age as his pa would have been. His leathery skin was wrinkled, and he had a shock of gray and white hair with a wispy mustache that matched. He still looked like a man not to be messed with, however.

Talbot stopped at a woodpile near the house, laid the shotgun on it, and looked up at the brothers on their horses. "If you boys need some help over at your place, you didn't need to mount up with pistols and carbines and put on your Sunday best to come ask me."

Moses chuckled. "We're gonna be deputy marshals, Sheriff . . . er, Mr. Jones."

The old sheriff gave a look of surprise, then grunted. "Well, don't that just beat all. Well, I can't tell if you're pullin' my leg or not, but if it's the truth, start workin' on not letting an old man with a shotgun get the jump on ya." He began moving toward the door.

"Mr. Jones, can we speak with you for a moment?" Elijah climbed down from his horse. Ever the cavalryman, Moses jumped down from his mount, took Bear's reins, and tied the horses off to a thin tree near the cabin.

"Lordy, just call me Talbot. You known me your whole life and are grown men." He walked inside the house, not inviting them but not closing the door.

Talbot walked past a small kitchen table, pulling out two chairs as he passed it. The brothers took it to mean they were invited to sit and watched the old sheriff pull a tin coffee pot away from the warm coals it was sitting over and fill three copper cups. The brothers nodded their thanks, and he returned the gesture before speaking.

"What's this about bein' marshals, then?"

Elijah looked at Moses, who just took a drink of his coffee. Elijah recounted Marshal Foster's arrival and request to the brothers and detailed the man the marshal was headed into Indiana to look for.

"Anyhow, we reckon this could be the same fella from the company in Pilot Knob, what with the playing card nonsense."

The old sheriff had pushed aside his coffee cup and just finished packing and lighting his pipe, a habit he had passed on to Elijah. "And so, what then, boys? You want my blessing? My advice?"

"Mr. Jones"—Elijah corrected himself—"Talbot. When our pa died fifteen years ago, you became like a father to us."

Moses snorted. "One of us at least," he mumbled.

Talbot stared at Moses, only turning back when Elijah resumed speaking.

"If not for you, I don't know what woulda become of us. You did what you could to help us keep that farm running, watched over us, took care of business for us in town . . ." Elijah trailed off, trying to portray a look of genuine thanks on his face, which was more emotion than he could usually muster. "All that when you was sheriff and still had a boy of your own." Elijah immediately grimaced at the use of *still*.

"It was the neighborly thing to do," Talbot said, puffing on his pipe. "Your pa was a good man; your ma helped out what with my boy not having a mother. You boys and him were about the same age." Elijah noticed a catch in his throat.

"We maybe can get some revenge for you and William," Moses whispered as if he was unsure that he should be saying it.

Elijah cringed at what was coming as Talbot slapped the table and stood up. "Golly, I thought your ma and pa, then me, raised you up smarter 'n this. Revenge? Some deviant pulls one over on you and that company, you all go off galavantin' after him instead of focusing on the war, get my boy and half a dozen other killed, and I'm supposed to listen to this nonsense about revenge? If it's even the same fella to begin with."

Moses looked at Elijah with anger, then back to Talbot. "I'm just saying that—"

Talbot cut him off. "Don't say nothing, Moses." He looked at Elijah. "Maybe I got an issue with your brother over what happened, but I also can't imagine the fix he was in, and all the things he did do for you all." He then sat down across from Moses and leaned across the table. "As for you, son," he said in his low, gravelly voice, "I'm sorry if you're upset I didn't treat you both exactly the same. He's the oldest; he was the one that had more responsibility. That's the way it works 'round here."

Moses sat back and turned his head away.

Elijah pushed back from the table and put his hands on his knees. "Mr. Jones, I'm sorry. I'm sorry for everything that happened, I'm sorry we came here and bothered you." He stood, put his hat back on his head, and Moses joined him. "We've already made up our minds though, so we'll be leaving this evening, regardless."

Talbot sat back with his mouth open. "You came to ask me to come with you, didn't you? Need someone with some actual lawman experience, so why not ask the old sheriff to come out for revenge, too?"

Elijah hung his head and didn't say anything.

"Foolish nonsense. All of it. Get out of my house, boys. You go on and do whatever you think it is you're doing, but you keep my boy's name out of your mouth about it."

With nothing else to say, Elijah nodded, walked out, and mounted his horse. The brothers crossed back over the stream to the trail and made their way toward the road in silence.

After a minute, Moses spoke up softly. "Well, at least that was some good coffee."

Elijah grinned again and shook his head. The enjoyment of a light moment passed quickly, though, at the thought of what he was leaving home to do.

He looked back at the old sheriff's cabin and thought he saw him watching them as they disappeared. Losing sight of the place as they rounded a bend in the tree line, Elijah put his legs to his horse. "Let's go find the marshal."

Opening Up

U.S. Marshal Solomon Foster and the newly deputized Elijah and Moses Barber took advantage of the long June day to begin their journey in the late afternoon. Hitting the state line five miles east of town, they ran into the Wabash River after another five and turned north, keeping the river on their right and the Toledo, Wabash, and Western Railway on their left. They eventually intended to cross over the river on their way toward Lafayette but decided to do so in the full light of the next day.

"I know you're probably wondering why we didn't just take the train," Marshal Foster said, "but I wanted to control our schedule and be able to poke around this part of the state and see what we could find. Plus, we've got some paper to serve along the way that may prove helpful."

"Ain't never gotta justify ridin' the open country to a couple of cavalrymen, Marshal," Moses said excitedly. "After five months home tryin' to make a farm work, this is good for the soul."

Elijah had to agree. The events near the end of their service had made him forget how much he missed this part. On top of a sturdy mount, riding the vast open ground, the creak of saddle leather, seeing nature. Most of all, just the relaxed conversation with others while not worrying about making ends meet. He was still uneasy around the marshal as he sorted out his measure of the man. Elijah didn't like that Foster had been prepared to take Moses alone but also understood the man had a job to do.

"That's Covington up there, just the other side of the river." The marshal was standing in his saddle, peering into the last of the day's light. The sun had tagged the horizon and was being sucked down as the endless sky filled with orange, pink, and red. "We've got some business there, but no sense trying to find the ford in the dark."

"Yessir," Elijah said. He nodded his head to the left at a tall, thick oak tree along the river, with some of its outer branches coming almost to the ground. "Nice flat spot there, with some grass and easy access to the water for the horses."

"I suppose making camp under the stars is another enjoyable activity for you cavalry boys?"

"Oh, c'mon now, Marshal. We know you infantry type weren't the adventurers we were, but surely you don't mind sleepin' on the ground?" Moses circled to the marshal and slapped him on the back.

"Well, I must admit, gentlemen," the marshal said sheepishly, "a regimental colonelcy due to your name and mostly focusing on administrative matters doesn't make you an experienced warrior."

"Nonsense, Marshal." Elijah sensed the man's modesty again but did not want it to become a liability. "You got an arm taken off by grapeshot; you are warrior enough, sir."

The marshal gave no reply as they dismounted and began setting up their camp.

AFTER WATERING THE HORSES and picketing them nearby in the thick summer grass, the men set out their bedrolls and made a modest camp. The warm day had become a cool night, but it was not so cool that it required fire for warmth. Enough fallen branches and twigs were about to construct a small cooking fire.

The men leaned back against their saddles; had some biscuits, beans, bacon, and coffee; and made small talk. Elijah noticed Moses seemed happy to be back in this element and had to admit it felt calming and familiar to him, too. Even the marshal, he sensed, seemed to be in his element. The marshal talked about his wife in St. Louis, Elijah lamented that he thought Sarah Jenkins was sweet on him and he hadn't said goodbye, and Moses asked if they'd visit any towns in Indiana that had dancing girls at saloons.

After finishing their meal, Elijah smoked his pipe while they looked at the endless sky full of stars of the clear summer night, and Moses pulled out his harmonica.

"Got it off a German feller from one of those immigrant regiments we were garrisoned with. My trusty mouth harp," he said. The other men laughed. He began playing "Kingdom Coming," a tune they all recognized from the war.

After a while, Moses played a final note, then began dragging his things to the other side of the tree. "Apologies, Marshal, but Eli knows. I don't like to sleep any closer to another smelly man than I need to. I'll see you in the morning." He gave Elijah and the marshal a mock salute and disappeared.

"He loves that song," Elijah said. "Played it all the time in camp. Said he liked to remember why we were fighting." Elijah turned and looked toward where Moses had retreated. "He'll be asleep in two minutes," he said with a chuckle.

The marshal laughed, and the two sat silently for a few minutes before he began again in a quiet voice. "You two have a complicated relationship, don't you?"

Elijah tapped out his pipe and stared into the darkness. "We do," he said.

"Tell me if I'm prying, but you said it was due to your relationship with the old sheriff, but it seems to have something to do with the war as well?"

"It does." Elijah let the statement hang in the air. He had no reason not to trust the marshal or open up to him. Still, it wasn't something he was accustomed to doing.

The marshal went quiet, apparently content to let it be.

Elijah heard Moses snoring and continued in a low voice. "He was my first sergeant when the bounty jumper killed our man and escaped." Elijah heard the marshal sit up at the revelation but remain silent, waiting to hear more.

"I put him in charge of a guard rotation overnight. Truth be told, it wasn't much of a concern. Sure, he'd been jumpin' bounties and cheatin' men at cards, but he hadn't been violent. Bit of a strange fella, but just figured keep a man on him to ensure he don't walk off again, leastways."

"Mmmhmm," the marshal uttered.

"Mo had been in line for a second lieutenant commission. We expected it any time. Once leadership found out what happened, though, they wanted a scapegoat and to make an example. Decided not giving the commission to the man that had been in charge of the guards was the way to go. He hadn't been negligent. I mean nobody could have predicted what would happen." Elijah looked down at the ground, picked a blade of grass, and tossed it. The image of the stabbed guard came to the front of his mind.

"He blames you then?"

"Yeah, or at least he used to," Elijah said. "For a while he always stewed that I should have stepped up for him more, then after a time

I think he just realized that was the way it was gonna go. Now he just prods me with it whenever he wants to get under my skin."

"Brothers, right?"

Elijah chuckled. "I reckon so. You have any?"

The marshal was quiet for a moment. "Both killed at Shiloh. They were a lot younger than me. Joined different regiments; didn't want big brother in charge of them. I suppose." He sighed. "They were always in a brigade nearby, though."

"Sorry to hear that, Marshal." Elijah was feeling out this new sensation of opening up to people. "You've seen some things, haven't you?"

"A burden I carry with me, Eli, but I know you do, too. What happened at Pilot Knob after he escaped?"

Elijah had figured it was only a matter of time until the marshal asked for the full story. "Well, I 'spose that's plenty why Mo and I have friction too . . ." He trailed off. "And with the sheriff . . . and the whole town."

The marshal was quiet, and Elijah continued.

"We got word General Price was movin' in; gonna try and take control of the town from us. This is all the day after the murder and escape. Heaviest fighting we'd been in so far, and we fall back to Fort Davidson. During the night, we get word from a prisoner that some local guerrillas coordinating with Price had snatched up one of our men who was off on his own. They think we might want to trade some of theirs for our man, not knowing he was a deserter prolly gonna be hanged."

Elijah poked a long branch at the dwindling fire, and it sparked up enough that he could see the marshal staring at him intently, allowing him to continue his story uninterrupted.

"Anyhow, we rode out, a few of us, under cover of having word of a vulnerable group of guerrillas, find the camp where the prisoner had said, and holler out we want our man back. We holler back and forth at each other with demands, insults going back and forth, not gettin' anywhere, and they threaten to kill him. I told 'em what he'd done and they'd be just savin' me the trouble hangin' him for me, and that I'd just go ahead and do the same to theirs and call it even."

"You didn't let it go, did you?"

"I surely did not," Elijah paused, his voice catching. "Mo told me we had bigger things to worry about, and our guy was gonna get what was coming to him either way. Sun was starting to come up, and we knew Price would be comin' at the fort. Smart play was to get back there."

Elijah watched a glowing ember lift from the fire and followed it into the expansive night sky, staring at the stars as he continued. "That's what happens when you put a farm boy who just knows riding and fighting in a spot like that, then have an escaped prisoner on his watch go and get his brother in trouble. Foolish." He paused and looked back at the marshal. "We went in after them, our man got away, and we killed half of their group and they returned the favor on six of mine. Made it back to the fort just in time to help hold Price off."

"Sheriff Jones's boy died shooting it out with the guerrillas, didn't he?"

"Yessir, he did. He was the one got clubbed half to death by our bounty jumper, then wouldn't take no for an answer goin' out lookin' for him." Elijah was quiet momentarily, staring at the stars. "Thing that keeps me up at night is that our colonel came to me with what they'd found out and said we ought just to hang him and be rid of the trouble. Said he had too much else to worry about."

"Hmm," the marshal uttered. "Well, I've taken the measure of you, Elijah Barber, and I imagine you didn't let him give that a second thought without letting him face his accusations. But I also know you must spend all sorts of time thinking how different things would be if you had."

The men were silent momentarily, the crickets and a bullfrog the only sound to be heard. Seeming to sense Elijah had exhausted his need to share, the marshal spoke up. "Well, Elijah, life is mostly in just how we react to hardships. I think you're on your way to a life of making peace and amends as you see fit. Plus, it seems like when it really counts, you and Moses are quite a team."

"When trouble brews up, or the bullets start flying, we are quite the team indeed."

The fire had died again, but Elijah heard the marshal situating under his blankets. "Well, I'm hoping I don't need your bullet flying abilities. We'll serve some papers and hopefully find this fella and his few hired guns. Hoping a badge and a couple rifles leveled at him brings his trouble making to an end. Get some sleep, Elijah."

"G'night, Marshal." Elijah stared up at the night sky once more. He sure hoped the man was right. He was sick of seeing killing and, more importantly, doing the killing.

The Ace

Twenty-five miles southeast—Rockville, Indiana

Frank Tucker stood leaning against the second-floor railing of the inn he now owned in his hometown, observing the dinner crowd. Little Rockville was straight south of Chicago, west of Indianapolis, and on the line from spots like Toledo and Cleveland toward St. Louis. The seat of tiny Parke County, the growing town of one thousand had potential.

He stroked his bushy beard. He saw few locals tonight, which didn't surprise him. They'd mocked his poor, ignorant father and then practically run him and his brother out of town. They joined the Union army to redeem themselves, and his brother was killed in the first fight they saw.

Bitter and full of rage, he turned to the bounty-jumping scheme, determined to return home, take what was his, and make a name for himself. He smiled and waved to a man named Warren, who was entering. Before the war, the man wouldn't have looked at him; now Tucker owned half his business. The man smiled meekly and awkwardly hurried his wife to their table.

With his gang of fellow deserters and a few other bitter locals, they'd started a series of fires around town, broke up some businesses, and generally attempted to run out the good folks, which they had mostly succeeded in doing. A town aiming to get a more significant piece of the railroad game needed commerce and the appearance of normalcy, however, and their violent tactics behind the scenes kept those who might challenge them in line.

Tucker allowed the local government just enough freedom to keep business carrying on and bring folks in for commerce within the county. When folks with money came, he let them be if they seemed ready to spend it or set up a business. If not, they fell victim to a "rotten string of thievery" the sheriff assured them he was working on, only to turn around and get his cut from Tucker. As far as the inn, tavern, and saloon Tucker was running went, he made sure the right palms got greased to look the other way from his goings on.

His thoughts were interrupted by his number two, Charlie Wade, coming up alongside him and leaning over the railing. Charlie was a short, stocky man. He had a face that most would consider quite handsome if not for the fact that his nose appeared to have been broken multiple times. He was clean-shaven and well-dressed otherwise.

The two men greeted each other, and Tucker pointed down at Warren. "I suppose we won't ruin a meal with his wife, but be sure to let Mr. Warren down there know this month's cut was lighter than expected again."

Wade grunted an acknowledgment. "One more month?"

"And nothing more," Tucker said. "Then the shop is mine." He gave a forced smile to another groveling patron down below. "What other news of the day, Charlie?"

"Went and saw the boys from the Greencastle robbery gone bad."

Tucker sighed. To allow some of his thicker-headed help to blow off steam, he'd often let them take small crews to knock off mercantiles and grocers for some money, with a cut to him. The risk seemed low, allowing him to see who was capable. However, the practice stopped after his men were arrested nearby with a suspicious amount of money.

"What of it, then?" He stood and pulled out a deck of cards and began shuffling.

"Well, Jack and Miles gonna be alright," Charlie Wade said, "but we had an issue with Tom."

Tucker stopped shuffling and raised an eyebrow.

"Well, I went in, and Jack and Miles are givin' me the look like they don't know me. So I ask after Tom, and the sheriff says no bail for him. I ask why, and the sheriff asks who I am. Told him I was his brother, here to bail him out and ensure he don't go runnin' with this crowd anymore."

Tucker smirked and continued shuffling.

"Anyhow, sheriff gets on telling me how my brother got mixed up in no good, fixin' for a life of trouble, and so forth. But good on him, he's gonna come back and testify against them to keep any paper off him and tell the court what happened—who else they're with and such."

"Seems Tom developed a knack for hide-saving stories," Tucker said. "Go on."

"Anyhow, the sheriff says the other two are gonna be kept for a trial. Said they had weapons found on them and the money and met the descriptions from a couple places. Don't know how Tom made his case." He paused and scratched at his face. "Bags on their faces, though, so that's a tough sell." Anyhow, I thanked the sheriff and made a big production out of saying how it's a good thing Tom is willing to come back as it seems the only way they'd be found guilty."

"Very clever . . ." Tucker trailed off as if anticipating the story's conclusion.

"So we get out of town, and I tell Tom that something doesn't seem right. I asked him if your name or anything about Lafayette or any other thing ever came out of his mouth, and he said no. Then he added that he might have talked *some*. Then he broke down and started askin' me if it'd be OK if he just didn't testify. I said of course and shot him."

"Charlie, how terrible," Tucker deadpanned.

"Anyhow. Jack and Miles mighta got caught, but they're sharp. If we send the lawyer over without the star witness, we'll have 'em back for you soon enough."

Tucker put the cards away and grabbed Charlie Wade by the arm. "Well done, well done. And you're right; they're good lads, and I have big things planned for them when they return." Straightening his jacket, he began to walk down the stairs, Charlie following. "I've been thinking about that railroad kid we met up in Attica, and I think we've been quiet long enough after Lafayette. Tell the men to stay sober; we'll leave later tonight."

Covington

—•—

Daylight came, and the marshal group had already had some coffee and leftover biscuits and was splashing across a ford into Covington. The small town of around one thousand mainly existed because of the railroad and because the county seat had to be somewhere. The men found the courthouse, slapped their reins to a hitching post, and walked inside to the office of the dual-hatted sheriff and town marshal.

"Mornin', fellas," said a portly man sitting at a small desk drinking coffee and reading a paper. He had sat upright rather quickly upon seeing the armed men, then relaxed again when he spied their badges. "What can I do for ya?"

"Name's Solomon Foster, brand new U.S. Marshal for the District of Indiana. These are my deputies, Elijah and Moses Barber."

Elijah and Moses both tipped their hats. Elijah looked around the small office, saw two small jail cells in the back, then looked at the empty desk he assumed was for a deputy.

The sheriff noticed him looking. "He's out on some business in the county, so just me today." He looked at Moses and then back at Elijah. "Brothers then? That's pretty neat." The sheriff didn't seem to have many visitors, especially not U.S. Marshals. "Name's Seth Taylor." He stood and gestured toward two chairs in front of his desk.

Marshal Foster sat and, in turn, gestured Elijah toward the other chair. Elijah could sense the glare from Moses as he leaned against a corner near the door.

"We got paper on a fella name of Dan Logan, Sheriff." The marshal pulled the warrant out of his suit pocket and slid it across to the sheriff, who studied it. "Was some holdover business from my predecessor. The word from some folks in Lafayette is he had shown up all drifter like a few days before that bank robbery. Trying to make nice with folks, asking all sorts of questions about the town."

Sheriff Taylor looked the papers over and scratched his head. Elijah didn't get the impression he dealt with such things very often.

"County sheriff got curious after everything that happened and went to the boardinghouse he was staying at to ask him some questions. Fella shot and killed someone and ran out back, stole a horse, and rode off." Marshal Foster removed another sheet of his paper from his pocket and studied it. "They found this in his room, looked sort of like a list of stops he was to make and meeting points. After Lafayette it said Attica, then Covington."

"So, you're thinking he's some sort of advance man for this fella robbing the banks?" asked the sheriff.

"That's right, Sheriff." Marshal Foster took the warrant back and replaced it with the other paper in his pocket. "Only other thing we know is that he'd been asking about blacksmith work in Lafayette and nearby towns. Don't rightly know if it was to blend in or what his angle was on that account."

The sheriff sat back and scratched the scruff on his face, then raised his eyebrows. "Well, Marshal. Goes by the name Will Greer, but we got a long-term boarder over at the inn kinda meets that description in the warrant. Showed up five, maybe six weeks ago and been workin' at the blacksmith. Talented fella."

"Well, advance man or not, he's a murderer and a horse thief. So, before we hang him for that, I'd like to see what he knows about the robbery."

"Now it's the marshal's job to set up and pay for a trial and all that, right? I don't got the resources to—"

Marshal Foster held up an exasperated hand. "Of course, of course."

"Will you take us to him, Sheriff?" Elijah wasn't sure what had motivated him to speak up, and he gave Marshal Foster an apologetic look.

Marshal Foster just smiled. "Was going to be my question exactly, Sheriff."

The sheriff put on his hat and led the men out into the street, nodding toward the inn a short distance away as they began walking in that direction.

Sheriff Taylor looked to Elijah as they walked. "You boys fight in the war? Saw the Spencers in your saddles."

"Yessir," Elijah answered.

"Thought you looked the part," the sheriff added. "How long you been deputy marshals now?"

"First day, Sheriff," Moses said eagerly.

The sheriff looked in disbelief at Marshal Foster, who just smiled, then looked at Elijah, who kept a straight face.

"Long story, Sheriff," Elijah said.

"Well, I reckon so," said the sheriff. He pointed to the inn's entrance and held out his arm. "Here we are, gentlemen."

The inn was a spartan one. A bare, wooden desk with some slots of keys behind it, a few tables and chairs in a sitting area, and stairs leading up to two hallways and twelve rooms. The sheriff walked to the front desk and rang the bell.

A very old man emerged from behind a curtain and seemed surprised to see so many armed men, then recognized the sheriff. "What can I do ya for, Sheriff?"

"Mornin', Vance. These fellas here are U.S. Marshals, got some paper out for a feller named Dan Logan."

The innkeeper Vance looked down at his log book and shook his head. "Nobody by that name, Sheriff."

"Didn't reckon so," the sheriff said as Elijah, Moses, and Marshal Foster poked their heads around. "How 'bout Will Greer? He still here? Thinkin' they might be one in the same."

The innkeeper's eyes lit up. "Oh, sure. Will is the best long-term guest I ever had. Pays on time; has helped me fix some things up. Talented fella. Said he wants to go out west and start his own shop in the goldfields after he saves enough. Only guest I got right this moment."

A door opened and shut upstairs, and a man came to the top of the stairs before looking down. He froze, then quickly retreated with a door slam soon following.

All four men had their guns out, and Marshal Foster went to the base of the stairs. "Dan Logan," Marshal Foster called out, "U.S. Marshals. We got a warrant to serve, and callin' yourself Will Greer or any other name won't do you any good."

Foster nodded at Moses, who slowly began ascending the stairs, but Elijah intercepted him, held up a hand, and continued up himself. Moses glared at Elijah, then followed a few steps behind.

Marshal Foster turned back to the sheriff. "Can you watch the lobby?"

The sheriff took up a position at the base of the stairs while Marshal Foster began cautiously climbing. Not quite to the top, Elijah whispered he'd start checking the rooms.

Moses and Marshal Foster braced themselves against the wall halfway up the stairs, where they could see both hallways out of sight. The marshal was breathing heavily and darting his eyes all over.

"Take a deep breath there, Marshal. This ain't worse than nything' we saw in the war," Moses said.

Marshal Foster pursed his lips and nodded before taking a deep breath.

Elijah entered the hallway they'd seen Logan duck back into. Gun held closely in front of him, he knocked on the first door and then kicked it in, peering into an empty room. Scanning the hallway and moving to the second door, he repeated the process to the same effect.

Arriving at the third door, he knocked, and just as he lifted his boot to kick the door in, a blast rang out, and the thin wooden door splintered into Elijah's face, knocking him to the ground. Dropping his gun, he screamed in pain, pawing at the bird shot and wood fragments stuck in his face.

Dan Logan stepped out of the room, a crying mess. "Ya'll shoulda just let me be," he babbled. Then he leveled the shotgun at Elijah's chest and cocked the hammer.

The Sheriff

Elijah didn't even hear the door at the end of the hallway swing open, but he heard two quick footsteps and the click of a hammer. Then, he heard a very familiar gravelly voice.

"Pulling that trigger would be a horrible mistake on your part, son."

Elijah looked up, thankful his vision was intact, and saw Talbot Jones holding a gun to the head of the shotgun-wielding man.

Moses had bolted to the top of the stairs, past Marshal Foster, who seemed frozen, and was leveling his gun down the hallway. "Hold it right there," he yelled at the shooter. "Drop it, and let me see some hands."

The man didn't comply quick enough for Talbot's liking, and he smashed the grip of his revolver across his face.

The man dropped the shotgun and brought his hands to his face as Moses stepped forward, kicked the gun aside, and pushed the man to the ground. "Eli, are you OK?"

Elijah nodded, then rattled his head to clear the ringing in his ears.

"Lord almighty, Mr. Jones." Moses lowered his revolver, shook his head, and patted the half-dressed old sheriff on his arm.

Talbot lowered the hammer on his revolver and stuck it in his waistband. "Will you not point that gun this way? And for the last time, Mo, call me Talbot."

Elijah was sitting with his arms on his knees and turned his head to Talbot, still trying to collect himself. He turned the other direction and saw Marshal Foster holster his revolver and walk their way.

Talbot helped Elijah up, then inspected his face before slapping him on the arm and moving toward Moses and Marshal Foster. Elijah stared at him for a moment, then shook his head and followed.

Talbot introduced himself to Marshal Foster, shook his hand, and asked Moses if he was OK.

"Oh, I'm fine. Just fine," he laughed. Elijah couldn't tell if it was nervous laughter or if he genuinely found the situation humorous.

"How the . . ." Elijah stumbled with his thoughts, still dazed by the incident. "What are you doing here?"

"That half-blind livery stable owner can't see worth a darn, but he sure runs his mouth. I got to feelin' bad, then realized I wasn't doin' anything else back home other than just stayin' alive, so I may as well keep lookin' out for you boys." He looked at each man. "Between your story yesterday and Benjamin's blabbering, I figured I'd find you soon enough."

"But you knew we were in Covington?" Marshal Foster was curious.

"Not 'specially. Just figured you hadn't made it much farther, so I forded the river just before dark and got a room. Ain't gonna sleep on the hard ground if I don't gotta."

The three camping companions from the night before looked at each other and smirked.

"Anyhow, figured I'd track you down this morning and help out. Good thing I did." He peered back at Logan or Greer or whoever he was. "You may want to actually tie him up or shackle him."

BACK IN SHERIFF TAYLOR'S office, Elijah sat at the empty deputy's desk while the town's doctor tended to his face.

"You're a lucky man," the doctor said as he removed pieces of wood. "Only see one ball stuck in your cheek; everything else is wood." He admired a particularly nasty-looking splinter before setting it aside. "The marks will look nasty for a while, and you'll have a scar from the pellet, but otherwise it'll heal up, I think."

Elijah winced and gave a small yelp as the doctor removed the piece of bird shot.

"Hell of a first day, Deputy." Sheriff Taylor had just stepped back in after locking the prisoner up.

The doctor stopped working and looked at Elijah. "First time getting shot on your first day as deputy. What a story."

"Not my first time getting shot," Elijah said.

"Right." The doctor looked from Elijah to the cavalry slouch hat sitting next to him, likely realizing what lawmen their age had been doing the last few years. The doctor removed the last splinter of wood, then applied some balm to a strip of cloth and dabbed it around the injuries. "Any higher and that eye would have been lost. Just keep it clean as you can, and you'll be alright."

Elijah nodded and muttered a thank you, then joined Marshal Foster and the sheriff at his desk, where the marshal had laid out some paperwork and a small notebook, after finishing a summary of where they were headed next. He had the sheriff sign the warrant where he'd made some remarks about what happened and what the man had told them.

"He says he wanted no part of the bank robbing scheme anymore and was trying to start a new life," Marshal Foster said. "Shooting at marshals didn't seem the right way to do that, but like you said, he'd been doing good work in town."

"Only life he's got now is a trial and waiting for a noose, I reckon," the sheriff said.

"Normally I'd stick around and get you a judge and court arranged," Marshal Foster said. "I'll send word on that, and we'll be back. But first we have to head to Attica. He said he never stopped there—as he'd been told—but thinks something big was supposed to happen there."

Marshal Foster wrote a document stating the costs for imprisoning the man would be covered and that trial arrangements would be made, and the men all stood and shook hands.

Stepping into the street, the group saw Talbot Jones finish securing a saddle bag and begin leading his gray quarter horse toward them.

Moses called out as Talbot neared them. "That horse born gray, Talbot, or get that way with you?" He laughed but turned serious when Talbot did not.

Talbot looked at Sheriff Taylor. "Well, Sheriff, I reckon I'm all square on pistol whipping that man back there."

Sheriff Taylor chuckled. "Well, sir, I didn't see it, but, that deputy there"—he nodded at Elijah—"vouched for it."

"He sure better have," Talbot said. He grinned faintly.

"Plus," Sheriff Taylor said, "the marshal here says you're with him, so that's good enough for me."

Talbot raised an eyebrow.

"Well, fellas"—the sheriff pointed north—"keep the river and the railroad in sight, and you'll run into Rob Roy in fifteen miles or so. Attica is another three miles north, right on the river. Attica been booming ever since the canal was completed 'bout twenty years ago. Rob Roy gets a little fussy that they missed out on the canal, and they only get the coal-hauling traffic, but it's a nice little town otherwise."

"Much obliged," Marshal Foster said, and the men all mounted up as the sheriff retreated into his office.

Sauntering out of town, a few curious eyes were on them, as word had gotten around about what happened. Some young boys eyed their horses and weapons when they stopped at the mercantile for food and supplies. Clearing town into the open country, Talbot spoke up, "So, I'm a deputy now, is it?"

Marshal Foster seemingly couldn't tell if Talbot was upset with him or if this was just his nature. "Well, I assumed since Elijah and Moses had asked, and then you had shown up . . ." He trailed off. "And now you're riding out with us."

"I don't gotta swear some kind of oath or something?"

"Marshal, this is just who he is," Elijah said.

"Talbot, Eli and me just stuck our hands up and said we'd uphold the law and follow orders and such. The marshal here said it's 'sposed to be more formal, but he just gave us badges and forwarded some paperwork."

Talbot laughed. "Well, Marshal, I done upheld the law before, and I'll do it again if it keeps these two alive. Don't matter if I got a piece of tin or not."

"Well, alright then," Marshal Foster said. "I think I've got one more badge in my saddlebag, I'll get it when next we stop."

They rode silently for a moment before Moses started laughing, and the group looked at him expectantly. "Ain't we just something to behold? A one-armed marshal, two brand new deputies, and an angry old man."

Talbot stared at him before laughing, and Marshal Foster joined him.

Elijah smiled as well, but inside he was worrying if they had bitten off more than they could chew. He touched the tender spots on his face and feared it wouldn't be the last of their injuries.

A Covered Bridge

The early summer day was one of the oppressively hot ones the part of the country kicked up occasionally without warning. With the sun high overhead, the group spied a low spot where the river bent to the right with a good shade tree stand. They watered then hobbled the horses in some good grass and decided to rest and let the day's heat pass.

Elijah had found a spot in the shade where the breeze blew across his face and was lying back against his saddle when he felt a kick to his boot. He looked up and saw Moses holding some bread and a piece of pork belly.

"Thanks, Mo," he said, sitting up and beginning to eat.

"I know you, brother. Just like after Pilot Knob, you woulda laid there feelin' sorry for yourself and questionin' your actions instead of eatin' nything." Moses also dropped his saddle in the shade and joined Elijah on the ground.

Elijah raised an eyebrow, then conceded his point. He offered his canteen to Moses, who thanked him but held up his own. Elijah glanced at Marshal Foster and Talbot, who were relaxing and conversing. "Looks like those two are getting on alright?"

"Oh, yeah." Moses laughed. "The marshal is tellin' war stories about Grant, and Talbot is givin' him every last piece of lawman advice he ever known."

"Still don't sit right to call him Talbot," Elijah said. He bit off a chunk of bread.

"Don't I know it," Moses replied, "but he gets more ornery every time I don't, so reckon I better get used to it."

They chuckled, then sat silently, enjoying the breeze and their modest meal.

"How you doin', Eli?"

"Oh, I'm alright, Mo. That sawbones in town said it'd heal up fine, save for a few scars."

Moses looked at him more seriously. "I don't mean that. I mean leavin' home; I mean all of this." He gestured around to the situation they'd found themselves in. "I ain't never seen you more unsure about makin' a decision, but the marshal said he ain't seen a man ever act so quick and confident like you did back at that inn."

"Lot of good that did me," Elijah said, pointing a finger at his torn-up face. "Dunno, though. Just saw that feller duck back in that hallway and something kicked in. Almost like a natural instinct. Someone tryin' to skedaddle from the law has somethin' to hide, ya know?"

"I coulda done it too, ya know?" Moses fixed a look on Elijah. Elijah thought it looked more like disappointment than anger.

"I know. I just . . ." He trailed off, looking around as if the words were somewhere in the prairie grass. "I'm tryin' to protect you, tryin' to remember I ain't the one in charge here. I'll work on it, Mo."

Moses nodded, then licked the remnants of his meal from his fingers and leaned back like Elijah. When Elijah thought they would settle in and rest for a bit, Moses spoke up again.

"It ain't your fault what happened back in Missouri, ya know. And you don't have anything ya need to prove or make up for."

Elijah opened his eyes and turned toward Moses, unsure where he was going.

"We can be out here 'cause we need to make a living, 'cause we want to be part of doin' something right with what skills we have, or just because we had to get out of Danville ..." He paused for a moment. "It don't have to be because you gotta fix some wrong, though."

"You sayin' I did wrong, then?" The comment didn't sit right with Elijah for some reason. He couldn't tell if Moses was sincere or trying to lecture him.

"No, Eli, I'm just sayin'—"

Elijah cut him off. "Don't be just sayin' anything to me then."

His exclamation was loud enough that it caused the other two men to look over at them.

Moses held up his hands and looked at the marshal and Talbot. "I was just pokin' fun at him about his face, and he got to fussin' back. We're all good."

Elijah shifted his saddle away from the other men and pulled his slouch hat over his face. "We're out here 'cause you wouldn't take no for an answer. And I don't need you savin' face for me with them, either—especially not when you wanna blame everything in life on me."

Moses gave an exasperated sigh and leaned back to get some rest. "You're the one changed his mind when you heard about the card—"

"Enough, Mo!" Without removing his hat or even turning toward Marshal Foster, he called out, "What time we movin'?"

He looked up at the bright sun beginning its descent toward the western horizon. "Let's give it another hour," Marshal Foster replied.

"Wake me when it's time, then," Elijah said. He didn't sleep, though. He thought about his mistakes at Pilot Knob, if he'd made any that morning at the inn, and wondered why he could never get things right with his brother.

THE GROUP RESUMED their travel as the sun continued toward the west, and they soon figured they were close to Rob Roy. They rode two by two, with Marshal Foster and Elijah in front. The pain in Elijah's face was tolerable, but he continued to feel sorry for himself as they plodded along. Moses called forward, breaking Elijah's trance of watching Bear's head bob.

"We gonna press to Lafayette tonight?"

Marshal Foster looked to the sky and then turned his head back. "I believe so, if we use all the light. Depends on how long we spend and what we find out, in Attica. We can get a real nice meal and a clean bed in Lafayette."

"Yessir, I'm lookin' forward to a city that size," Moses said. He was grinning from ear to ear. "I bet they got a saloon and some pretty girls to go with that meal."

Talbot looked over at him and shook his head, then called forward. "What then in Lafayette? After the meal and young Mo here blowin' his pay 'fore, you even give it to him, that is."

"Well, Sheriff, we'll speak with the local law, the folks from the bank, and anyone else that might help us find this fella and his gang." Elijah noticed that the marshal had taken to calling Talbot sheriff, and Talbot never corrected him as he did with Moses and him.

Talbot stretched in his saddle, bit his lower lip, and spoke up again. "I know I was an add-on to all this and was just a local lawman myself, but this fella, whoever he is, has gotta be long gone, right?"

The marshal was quiet for a moment before answering. "Well, that certainly is likely. But we gotta start somewhere, and Lafayette was the last place he popped his head up."

Talbot appeared to consider this, then only nodded without a reply. Elijah couldn't see him but took his questioning to mean he was impatient and unsure of the plan. But Talbot's lack of further response meant he thought it was the best plan.

As they neared the town of Rob Roy, Elijah noticed it was set to the east of the railroad tracks and river by maybe two or three miles. He spotted two or three covered bridges spanning what must have been a substantial stream branching off from the Wabash, and that was likely why the location was chosen for the town. Up ahead to the west, he could see a southwest-bound locomotive heading their way.

Elijah's admiration of the bridges and train was disturbed when they heard the squealing and screeching of it coming to a sudden stop.

"Thought that fat sheriff said it didn't stop in Rob Roy?" Moses sat up in his saddle and strained to look. "Ain't even a station there, and it don't look like a coal carrier."

The four men had stopped and were using their hands to shield their eyes from the low sun when they heard the report of a gunshot. They all reached for their revolvers, and Marshal Foster began a trot toward the train. The others followed.

Just north of the town, they saw four men on horses ride out from inside one of the covered bridges, make a hard left and begin to canter toward the train. When the men from the bridge had covered half the distance to the train, the marshals heard gunfire coming from inside. Two of the bridge riders continued to advance on the train, firing as they did, while the other two suddenly turned toward Marshal Foster and his men.

Marshal Foster stopped, seemingly considering what to do about the situation. That's when Elijah saw one of the men raise his arm and, a second later, heard the familiar hiss and snap of a ball passing just by his head.

The Train

Elijah Barber flashed back to the battlefield when the ball narrowly missed his head. "They're shooting at us!" Elijah yelled.

"We don't know who they are shooting at or who they are," Marshal Foster replied.

Elijah squinted at the approaching riders. "Do honest folks cover their faces and shoot at strangers?"

Marshal Foster gave no reply, and when he seemed to be hesitating, Elijah instinctively took command.

Jerking his horse to the right, he yelled, "Mo, let's get on either side of them! Marshal, you're with me."

Elijah kicked Bear in the ribs and shouted encouragement as he led the marshal off to the right, knowing Moses was dragging Talbot in the opposite direction. Straightening out their direction of travel, he looked across to Moses and Talbot, seeing them do the same. The three groups of riders formed a closing triangle, with the riders from the covered bridge forming the point on top.

He hoped Bear and Copper weren't gun-shy and were up to the task. He gave the buckskin a few firm pats on the neck. "Alright, Bear. Here we go, boy."

Elijah saw his brother pull his carbine from the scabbard and did the same. Yanking the reins to the left, Elijah levered a round into the chamber. Moses fired first, the rider closest to him jerking upward and falling off the back of his horse.

Elijah fired and saw his target's shoulder turn as he worked the lever and fired another round, finding the rider's chest as both horses raced past them. Wheeling their mounts around, Talbot got to the slumped-over rider, whose horse had slowed, and pulled him down from the saddle as the man groaned loudly. He tried to raise his weapon, and Talbot dispatched him with his revolver.

The brief victory was short-lived as the cries from the railroad turned the marshal and his deputies' attention back to the train. Circling up around each other, Talbot said that he saw a group of riders had come up from the riverbank on the far side of the train.

"Counted five or six on horse, before I lost sight. Looked like two or three riderless horses as well. I reckon they got men on board."

"Robbing a train?" Elijah looked at Marshal Foster, who was decidedly distressed. "Has such a thing ever happened?"

"Not in peacetime," he said. His voice was shaking.

"What's the plan, Marshal?" Talbot stared at him, seeming to want him to take the opportunity to lead his group.

Marshal Foster spun his horse around and saw shooting coming from inside the train to the riders outside, felling one of them.

"Marshal, I'm not sure who's shooting from inside the train," Elijah said, "but I reckon we can run off this one remaining fella on our side then use the train as cover to see what's going on."

The marshal hesitated to answer, and Elijah realized he must take control.

"Marshal, if ever something was federal jurisdiction, it'd be a train getting robbed." He didn't wait for an answer, slapping legs to his horse and galloping off toward the train with Moses in close pursuit.

Seeing the two men coming, the last remaining rider on the east side of the train rode to the back and went up and over the tracks to join the rest of his gang. Moments later, Elijah heard two rapid-fire reports and more screaming. Arriving at the tracks, he and Moses put their carbines back in the scabbards, dismounted, and pulled out their revolvers as Marshal Foster and Talbot rode up.

Elijah handed his reins to Marshal Foster and gestured for Moses and Talbot to do the same. Not wanting to hurt his feelings, Elijah told him it was part of any cavalry battle for one man to hold three horses. "If anyone comes through to this side again, you'll shoot at them and let us know what's happening."

The group heard doors of cars sliding open opposite them and the occasional yell or shriek from passengers inside. The shooting had stopped for now, but he heard quite a scuffle in the passenger car and the one ahead of it.

"That's the last bag," they heard a voice yell. "Go! Go!" Then there was a loud thumping noise.

There was some yelling, and then crossing over the tracks, in front of the locomotive, and away from them, a group of five riders with flour sacks over their heads took off at a hard gallop to the south. Moses began to reach for his carbine, but Elijah stopped him.

Elijah motioned for Talbot to creep toward the front of the train while Elijah and Moses slid along the side of the passenger car where all the commotion had come from, making their way to the door in the back. The only sound was the pings and hisses of the stopped locomotive until they were spotted from inside.

"Got two comin' 'round back, boss!"

Moses reached the steps first, grabbing the handle and swinging onto the platform, pushing through the door with Elijah behind him. Entering the car, they saw two bodies in the aisle; one was face-up and had a badge on his chest. Standing at the front was a man with a covered face holding another in an arm lock with a gun to his head. A handful of cowering and screaming passengers began huddling behind them.

"That's close enough or this unfortunate passenger gets it," the bandit said.

Elijah lowered his gun only slightly, and Moses did the same. He looked at the masked man in time to see him cock his head as if in recognition.

"Captain Elijah Barber," the man said in a cold and calculated voice. "With a deputy marshal badge on his chest? If I had spent the last nine months making up a story, I could not have done this well."

The Pinkerton

The man looked from Elijah to Moses, then out the door to the ground. "How's that safe looking?"

"We might need to leave it, boss."

He moved with the hostage toward the door while Elijah and Moses whispered to passengers to move behind them and out the door in the back.

The hostage taker stood on his toes and peeked out the window while he watched the passengers exit. "Tell your men out there that those people are safe so long as they stay there and don't try anything." He turned out the door to the ground again. "You hear that?"

Moses went to the window and spoke to Marshal Foster and Talbot while Elijah kept his gun on the bandit.

"I see you're still firmly on the side of what is right and expected, Captain," the man said. His tone was mocking. "As you can see, I've chosen a bit of a different path. Although I assume bounties are still involved."

Elijah had lain awake most nights since Pilot Knob, thinking about what he would say if he ever had the occasion to see this man again, but he was unsure of himself in this situation that he could have never predicted.

"Marshal," Elijah called over his shoulder, "why don't you get those people headed across the field into town and away from this train."

"Elijah," the marshal called in, "I can't see what's happening in there, but we've got these people safe, and it's your call as a sworn deputy."

"Sworn deputy," the bandit echoed. His voice was full of disdain.

"How we gonna do this?" Elijah was stalling for time, allowing Marshal Foster and the passengers to get distance from the train. "What am I even calling you?"

"I'm not sure I even remember what name I was using when last we met," he added.

"Thomas Locke," Elijah said, matter-of-factly.

"If you say so, Captain."

"Deputy Marshal now."

"How I bore of the semantics," he said. He made a yawning noise. "Surely the fine passengers have well and cleared the area. Put your guns down, I hop down to the ground, my companion and I mount up with the passenger here, and once I'm clear, I drop him off."

"Eli," came Talbot's voice from outside, "I got a gun in my back out here."

Elijah stepped forward and looked past the thief to the ground outside the train. Nobody was there, and he realized the thief had been pretending to talk to someone while they had crept around to Talbot instead.

The thief grinned and backed down the steps out of the car, pulling the passenger with him.

Elijah and Moses moved quickly to the steps and out onto the ground, their guns trained on him.

"Do whatever you need to do, Eli," Talbot shouted over the noise of the chuffing locomotive.

"Alright, you can let him go then," Elijah said. "Take your man his horse, leave me the passenger and our man, and we let you ride off."

The train robber nodded. "That's fine. Just know it won't turn out well for you if you do decide to give chase." He shoved the passenger, sending him stumbling forward to the ground, then doffed his bowler hat and walked backward to where the horses were, keeping his gun trained on Elijah and Moses. "Good luck with your new profession, Captain." He moved around to the front of the train, and Elijah soon heard the hoofbeats of their departure.

"You still with us, Talbot?" Elijah shouted. Moments later, he saw a disgruntled-looking Talbot Jones walk around the front of the train. Relieved, Elijah turned to the man who had been a hostage. "Sir, are you alright?"

The man was shaking, but he nodded. Talbot took him by the arm and began leading him back around the train and toward town.

Moses walked over to the safe and picked up a bag lying nearby. "Well, I guess they didn't get it all, at least." He reached inside and made a pained face. Moses dumped the bag out, and Elijah saw two playing cards float to the ground.

"Aces?" Elijah kicked at the cards with his boot, saw he was right, and threw his hat on the ground.

Moses suddenly looked up with alarm, and Elijah saw him draw his gun. Elijah whirled and did the same and saw a lone mounted man barreling toward them. The brothers both raised their revolvers.

"Friendly!" the man was shouting. He slowed the horse and raised his hands. "Friendly, I'm friendly."

Elijah and Moses approached the foaming and panting horse, one on either side with their guns raised. "Alright, mister," Elijah said, "hop down with your hands where I can see them."

The man swung down slowly, his hands in the air. "May I pull aside my coat and show you my badge?"

"Better be real slow like, mister," Moses replied.

"Name's Matt Hobbs, Pinkerton National Detective Agency." He slowly pulled aside his jacket to reveal the badge. "My partners are inside the passenger car." He attempted to look forward into the car.

Elijah nodded gravely, then shook his hand. "Elijah Barber, and this is my brother, Moses." He immediately regretted looking like an amateur and not better identifying themselves. "We're deputy U.S. Marshals," he added for good measure, delaying the inevitable of delivering the news.

"I take from the look on your face, that they did not fare well."

"They did not," Elijah said, lowering his head and wishing there had been a better way to tell him.

The three men stood awkwardly for a moment before they heard a shuffling in the front of the train, and they pulled their revolvers.

"Don't shoot," came a terrified voice, followed by some hands emerging from the window. The train conductor's head soon followed.

Elijah holstered his revolver and stepped toward the locomotive. He asked the conductor if he was alright and conferred with him briefly regarding what had happened and what he should do next.

"You got any help in there?"

"Got an engine man in here that soiled himself and is just this side of useless."

"Understandable," said Elijah. "He able to help you get this thing switched off onto the coal train siding after you back it up some? Then you can join us in town."

The conductor nodded and disappeared back inside, and the men soon heard the slumbering locomotive come to life and begin moving backward.

"We'll get some men sent out to bring your partners in," Elijah said, uncomfortable that there was nothing else to be said or done about it.

"Yeah," Hobbs replied.

"Our marshal took the horses with him when he escorted the passengers." Elijah gestured toward Rob Roy, making clear he intended to head there.

"I'll walk too, then," Hobbs said. "The horse needs a break anyway." They began walking, and the Pinkerton asked, "Mind my wondering why the marshal bugged out and left just the deputies?"

"Only got one arm," Moses said quickly, as if nothing about that was unusual.

Hobbs snorted but then looked at Elijah and saw he was serious.

"And it's only our second day on the job," Elijah said.

The Pinkerton stared at Elijah in shock, then looked to Moses. "I might find all that highly amusing were the situation not so serious," he said. "It appears we need to catch each other up," he added.

BY THE TIME they reached the town, Elijah and Moses had caught the Pinkerton up on the early exploits of their unlikely group, and the all but confirmed personal connection they had to the man they had started calling Ace. They gave Hobbs their story since leaving Danville, right up through Elijah's injury from the morning and the events of the train robbery.

"Picked the right day to find that fella in Covington, I guess." Hobbs shook his head at the timing.

"Lot of good it did us," Moses said. "We got more trouble now than when we set out."

Detective Matt Hobbs explained how the Merchants Bank in Lafayette had hired the Pinkerton Agency to track down the man they assumed was Ace and how they had traveled from Chicago to begin piecing things together.

"They also told us to link up with the new U.S. Marshal, once he was in place," Hobbs said. "So, I guess we . . . ," he trailed off, then corrected himself. "Guess I have accomplished that now, too."

The group discovered the small inn hosting the displaced train passengers. Marshal Foster had been moving among them, gathering information, and hurried over to his men when they entered, relieved they were OK.

Elijah caught the marshal up, then Hobbs continued his narrative.

"Anyhow, we get the story from the folks in Lafayette about them coming through the day Lincoln's train did, the early morning robbery, the strangely calm man with the cards, and him shooting the marshal and leaving the playing card."

"Guess we don't need to head to Lafayette now," said Marshal Foster.

"All we got out of askin' around town was that some folks had seen a man skulking around town asking questions the day before." He held out a hand to Elijah, indicating that it matched his story about Covington. "The only other info we got was that the bank assistant and a few others confirmed they rode southwest out of town. We made our way to Attica, hoping we were following them, but no sign."

"So, what kept you in Attica?" Talbot asked, seeming to step back into his investigative lawman persona.

"Asked some kid at the Attica station if he'd seen a group of men might fit the description. Kid immediately gets all wobbly and can't keep a story straight. Didn't even have to get aggressive with him; just gave it all up. Some mellow talking man in a bowler hat gave him a few double eagles to say he never saw them and to help them with something at the station when they came back in a few weeks."

"What'd they want him to do?" Marshal Foster asked.

"Just said to let them on, keep his mouth shut, and if everything went well, the man would tell him where to find him if he really wanted to make some money. So, we told the kid to keep the money, doubled it from us, and told him to signal us if and when the day came. We were about to leave town when the kid sent a signal they were there."

Hobbs wrapped up his account by detailing that they watched two men milling around the train station just before departure, so he and his partners kept a low profile, and his partners boarded like regular passengers. Ace's crew jumped on at the last second. "I stayed back in case he had any men that did so as well . . ." He trailed off and was silent for a moment. "I should have been with them."

"Your men did some fighting while they could, for whatever that counts," Moses said.

Hobbs just nodded. "We had it close to figured for a while and ended up with two dead. You all caught a last-minute break and took a few of them out." He chuckled. "Funny how things play out."

Marshal Foster interjected, "I believe we'd all better head into Attica and talk with the boy and their justice of the peace and get on the same page."

"You gonna join up with us?" Elijah looked at Hobbs, unsure of the protocols for Pinkertons and U.S. Marshals working together but hoping he'd say yes.

"We'll deputize you if we need to," Marshal Foster said. "For now, we'll be glad to have someone working to the same end."

"When I get to Attica," Hobbs said with a stone-cold serious look, "I aim to send word back to Chicago and Lafayette, gather my things, and head after this man, whether it's with you or not."

Attica

Deciding to head back up the line to Attica, the conductor said he could slowly back the train up that far and offered a ride to save time as the day's light had run out. Marshal Foster took him up on it, and Detective Hobbs decided it best to take the dead Pinkertons back to the bigger town where their belongings were to make arrangements.

"I covered them fellas up in the passenger car best I could," the conductor said, still trembling. "I didn't know what else to do." The men all agreed with his actions as they climbed into the small car that had held the mail, various bags, and the safe some folks from town had helped reload. As they began backing up toward Attica, Marshal Foster was writing furiously at a small desk, and Elijah said he would take some air during the short trip.

Stepping outside to the small platform, he leaned against the railing, listening to the train in the otherwise quiet night. Hobbs soon joined him outside.

"Hopefully they don't know I'm out here to talk about them," the Pinkerton detective said in a low voice.

Elijah raised an eyebrow.

"I'm not some kind of expert of personalities and such, but between my time in the war and on this job, I know who's in charge when a group of men are doing dangerous work and who isn't."

Elijah nodded and considered this. He liked and wanted to trust this man. Hobbs was handsome, with trimmed hair and a well-groomed mustache that extended beyond his lips and down to his chin. He wore a suit similar to himself and Moses, but it fit him better. The pocket watch and chain in his vest and how he carried himself revealed he had more exposure to high society than Elijah. "You fought in the war, then?" Elijah asked.

Hobbs removed a small cigar from his pocket, offered another to Elijah, who declined, and pulled out his pipe. "Cavalry in the Army of the Potomac. Got assigned early on escorting around this spy McClellan had brought in."

"Pinkerton?" Elijah asked, puffing on his pipe.

"The man himself." Hobbs made a grand gesture with his hand holding the cigar. "Thought I'd been resigned to babysit some paper pusher running all over counting troop numbers and talking to assets, but"—he puffed on the cigar—"well, you've heard the stories, I'm sure. Plus, it landed me a job after."

"Truth be told," Elijah said, "I'm a bit ashamed to admit I only just learned of him and his agency."

Hobbs looked at Elijah, surprised.

"Well, when you spend your whole life on a central Illinois farm, then fight in the Missouri backwoods, you miss a lot of the goings on of the world."

"Fair enough." Hobbs grinned. He then gestured at the faint appearance of Attica up the track. "Your group, then?"

"Well, you already know the story with Locke, or Ace, or whatever we're calling him—"

"Which still astounds me," Hobbs interjected.

"Yes, well, there's plenty more." He took a long puff on the pipe, then detailed their long relationship with Talbot Jones and spoke of the botched retrieval attempt at Pilot Knob and that Talbot's son was killed during it.

"So, the old man felt too tired for revenge but got stirred up by you two wanting it for him and has some deep sense of duty to care for you?"

Elijah nodded. "Something like that."

"I get why he's here then, and I understand the marshal's background, but he's not in charge, Eli."

Elijah cocked his head.

"Formally, yes," Hobbs said. He held a hand up in defense of his point. "I saw it from the first instant, however, that your brother and the old sheriff look to you." He finished the cigar and tossed the butt off the now-slowing train. "I believe Foster does, too."

"Oh, I don't know." Elijah tapped out his pipe.

Hobbs hopped down with Elijah to give himself another moment to speak as the others departed the train. "I watched your brother tell everyone how you went into action when the shooting started, and let me tell you, Eli. I saw a lot of men telling action stories of men they admired during the war, but I never saw one with as much admiration as he showed."

The door of the train opened, and the other three men emerged. Seeing Elijah, then looking at the town of Attica, Moses said, "Well, brother, it ain't Lafayette, but it'll do for the night." He hopped down and slapped Elijah on the back.

Elijah saw Hobbs smile at him out of the corner of his eye.

THE BOY THAT ACE, then the Pinkertons, had spoken to previously was a blubbering mess when the men reached him at the Attica train depot. Elijah didn't think he could have been more than thirteen or fourteen.

"Has he done something wrong? Did he have something to do with all this?" An older man had stepped out of an office and was staring at the boy as he asked the questions. The group soon realized he was the station manager and the boy's father.

"Indirectly," Hobbs said.

The older man's face hardened, and he lunged for the boy.

"Alright, mister," Moses said, holding him back. Elijah noticed Talbot leaning against the door frame, grinning. Whether at Moses's intervention or admiring the wrath of a father figure, Elijah wasn't sure.

The man took a seat, and Marshal Foster explained what they knew about the boy's involvement and that they just needed to ask a few more questions. The father had been concerned when he saw his town's justice of the peace was involved and blown up again when he realized U.S. Marshals and the Pinkerton Agency were also involved.

"Your boy did the right thing, once we explained what might be at stake," Hobbs said. He winked at the boy as if to indicate his lips were at least sealed regarding the double eagles from him.

"Son," Marshal Foster began, "did they say anything about their plan, when they came back into town?"

Elijah noticed Marshal Foster was much more in his element in the quiet, sorting-out-the-facts moments.

The boy wiped the tears and snot from his face and put on a brave face. "He asked me if I said anything, and I told him no. But he mighta known I was lying, because he started looking around. But then he started askin' me if I knew what I was loading up at the stop, when exactly the train would leave, how many people on board, and such."

"And that's when you sent word to us that the man had returned?"

"Yessir. Told my friend Paul, who sometimes helps me load and unload, that I'd give him one of the gold coins if he'd run and tell ya."

Elijah raised his eyebrows and grinned at the little schemer.

"Where's Paul now?" The father was nearing fury again at the situation.

"No idea, Pa."

"Smart kid," Moses chuckled.

"I'll leave that to you," Marshal Foster said, turning to the Attica justice of the peace who had met them when they arrived. He turned back to the boy. "Son, did they say where they were going? What they planned next?"

"He told me"—he looked at his father, fearful of what he'd say next—"that a boy shouldn't let his father hold him back. That if I wanted to collect my share for helping and start earning what I deserved, to come find him."

The father gave a horrified look, but Detective Hobbs interjected. "That's likely just what this fella tells himself, and how he recruits, sir. Don't let that stick in your craw." He turned back to the boy. "Where'd he say to find him?"

The boy ran a hand through his hair and contorted his face, trying to think. "Rockton...? Rockville!"

The men all turned to the Attica justice of the peace expectantly. "South of here a spell; can't say I know how far, exactly." The marshal scratched his head. "Think it's along the Indiana and Illinois Central. Sheriff Taylor will know better 'n me."

They all thanked the father and the boy and stepped outside. Elijah saw Hobbs check his pocket watch and raise an eyebrow.

"Just after nine," the detective said.

"Now or in the morning, boss?" Moses asked. He tapped his fingers on his holster, inadvertently advertising that his blood was up.

Marshal Foster and Detective Hobbs simultaneously answered "Morning" and "Now," emphasizing the unclear chain of command and the difference in opinions.

"We can only assume after how this went that they know the boy talked and would have told us where they were," said Marshal Foster.

"And right now, they're riding hard; won't have time to prepare for a fight—might even figure we'd wait until daylight," Hobbs countered.

"If they're even going there," Talbot added stoically.

The group all turned toward Elijah, and he realized what Hobbs had been trying to tell him earlier about being the "action" leader. He felt uncomfortable with that arrangement and, worse yet, was having panicked thoughts about the last time he made a rushed decision when trying to track someone down.

"We should get some rest, make sure the horses are fresh and that we're supplied," Elijah said. "Leave very first thing and check in with the sheriff in Covington and try to get a lay of the land. We'll be in better shape to plan if we do all that."

The men all gave their ascent, Hobbs begrudgingly so.

"I can send some fellas to retrieve your horses and gear in Rob Roy," the peace officer said. "We'll get 'em tended to and let you fellas relax. Tavern has some food ready for ya and a few rooms."

"Much obliged," Marshal Foster said, leading his group toward the still-lit corner building on Main Street.

Hobbs hung back, waiting for Elijah, then began to walk alongside him. "See what I mean?"

Elijah chuckled and shook his head. "Guess I'd better get used to it," he said. "Sorry I went against you."

"Not at all," Hobbs said. He put a hand on Elijah's shoulder. "A good leader hears it all out and makes a decision. Let's get some chow and see if this place has anything harder than coffee to drink."

"I think we need it," Elijah replied.

New Destination

The telegraph tapped to life early in the morning, and the operator quickly made his way to the inn and delivered the message.

"Anything from Chicago?" asked Hobbs.

The telegraph worker shook his head and then looked to Marshal Foster.

"I hadn't told him to be awaiting anything," Marshal Foster said.

Elijah saw Hobbs frown at the marshal.

Taking the handwritten note in hand, Marshal Foster mumbled through some of it before skipping around as he read aloud, "Proceed with all caution to Rockville . . . verify identity . . . arrest if sufficient evidence." He looked at the group. "It's something at least."

The men all nodded as they ate a hurried breakfast that the tavern owner had been compelled to put forth with some economic encouragement. "Everyone, gather your things. We'll meet at the livery, shortly," Marshal Foster said.

Elijah looked outside to see the very beginnings of an orange glow coming up over the horizon. He saw Matt Hobbs holstering a revolver he had retrieved from his belongings. "No word from your people, then?"

Hobbs put on and straightened his jacket while glaring at Marshal Foster. "Apparently not." He looked at Elijah. "Does the marshal always just ignore anything that isn't his own idea or concern?"

Elijah felt uncomfortable answering the question, especially in light of their leadership discussion from the day before. "Oh, I don't know—"

Hobbs waved a hand. "No matter. Regardless, I'm continuing on after this Ace fellow. I owe it to that bank to see about getting some of their money back, to those men for avenging their death, and to the agency for both. I suppose the railroad now, too."

"I admire your conviction," Elijah said, putting on his jacket in preparation to depart.

The group saddled their horses at the livery, paid for the services, and thanked the Attica justice of the peace as they departed south at a trot for the two-hour ride to Covington.

Arriving in Covington just after eight a.m., Elijah suggested they take their horses to the livery again. "Sounds like we'll have thirty miles or more to go today, and I don't think it'll be relaxing when we get there. The cavalryman in me says we want those horses as cared for as can be."

Moses and Hobbs agreed adamantly, and the group asked the stable hand to feed and water the horses while they went to talk to the sheriff.

As he had been the day before, he was reading his paper and having his coffee, but he reacted much more quickly this time at the group's stern arrival and spying a Pinkerton badge on a new man.

"Never thought I'd have a Pinkerton in my office," Sheriff Taylor said. He shook Hobbs's hand after being introduced. "I reckon you aren't just on a goodwill tour of Fountain County?"

"No sir," Hobbs said, "but my work and that of Marshal Foster's collided quite violently last evening."

The sheriff's expression turned grave, and he gestured to the chairs in front of his desk, then pulled over some more. "I'm afraid I only have the four," he said, looking at Talbot leaning against a window sill.

Talbot waved him off. "Best to spare everyone the spectacle of me tryin' to get back up out of it after all this time in and out of the saddle." The men all chuckled, but the moment of fun was short-lived.

"Sheriff, Mr. Hobbs here was looking for the same man we were," Marshal Foster began, "and by God if we didn't all find him yesterday."

Sheriff Taylor scanned the expressions of all the men seated before him and very likely already deduced it was not a pleasant encounter. Marshal Foster went on to detail the train robbery, the men they had to kill, and the interaction on the train and subsequent getaway.

"Injuries for you guys?" Sheriff Taylor looked around the room, only noting Elijah's same injuries from the last time he saw him.

"None of ours," Marshal Foster said quietly, "but—"

"They killed two of mine on the train," Hobbs interjected flatly.

The sheriff sat back, running a hand through his hair and taking this all in. "Well, I'm mighty sorry to hear that, Mr. Hobbs."

Hobbs dropped his head and nodded, mumbling a thank you.

"Sheriff Taylor, how far a ride is Rockville?" Elijah asked the question abruptly and immediately realized he was stepping into the marshal's territory again, seeming impatient to get moving.

Marshal Foster sighed and shifted in his chair but said nothing and awaited an answer.

Elijah saw what he thought was a look of approval from Hobbs out of the corner of his eye.

The sheriff raised an eyebrow, then looked to be thinking. "Follow the river maybe twenty miles to Montezuma, then follow the Indiana and Illinois east"—he scratched his chin—"oh, another five miles or so." He paused momentarily, then added, "From what folks who've been through there recently say, they been having an awful mess of a time down there."

"Sounds about right," Moses said, glancing around at the group.

Marshal Foster filled in the rest of the details they'd gathered from the boy in Attica, and Sheriff Taylor finally understood why they were asking about Rockville.

The men all sat quietly for a moment, and Elijah noted that the sheriff was not volunteering to come with them, even after what had gone down in his county. Marshal Foster and Sheriff Taylor began conferring about the route to Rockville, and Elijah said he would take some air. He nodded toward the door at Moses and tapped Hobbs on the shoulder as he walked out.

Elijah stepped outside onto the boardwalk and began stuffing his pipe as Moses and Hobbs joined him.

"He sure don't wanna go," Elijah said, lighting the pipe and beginning to puff on it.

"That much is true," Moses said.

"I don't know what Foster is thinking," Hobbs said, "but he sure has a case of the slows. If he'd been a commanding general, old Abe would have fired him like my first boss."

Elijah could see that the Pinkerton would vote yes for going after Tucker immediately. "You reckon waiting for any help just allows him to either dig in or fully skedaddle?"

"That's exactly what I think," Hobbs said.

"How 'bout you, Mo?" Elijah looked at his brother while puffing on his pipe.

Moses nodded down the street toward a hardware store and a mercantile. "I reckon we ought to see what they got for ammunition and weapons in them stores," he said. Turning to Hobbs, he added, "I'd like to see another repeater in the hands of our new Pinkerton friend here."

Elijah was tapping out his pipe, preparing to head back inside, when Talbot stepped out into the sun. "What are you boys out here gossiping about?"

"Talbot, anyone ever tell you what a delightful disposition you have?" Moses laughed.

Talbot squinted into the morning sun. "If we ain't goin' after this fella, then what a waste of a trip this was. Other than saving Elijah's behind, that is."

Elijah grinned. "We were just about to go over yonder and see about some guns and ammunition," he told Talbot. "Figured we'd let the marshal know our vote that way and see about a repeater for the Pinkerton here."

"You boys load up all you want on your fancy weapons; I'll be just fine with my revolver and the scatter gun." He turned his head inside the door. "Marshal, the cavalry is out here fixin' to go gear up with the quartermaster unless you're figurin' different." He turned back to the group. "Maybe get some food and provisions too, fellas? Don't weigh yourself down with ammunition only, Moses."

"Yessir," Moses replied.

Elijah heard a chair scrape on the wood floor, and Marshal Foster appeared in the doorway. He laid out their options, then asked around the group. "Everyone thinks we should move in, then?" He looked from man to man, getting nods all around. "Get whatever supplies you need, and we'll meet at the livery. We'll go find this Ace."

Elijah and Hobbs began walking toward the store together.

"More leadership by consensus," Hobbs said, "presented as bold decision making."

Elijah was growing increasingly concerned their worries over Marshal Foster's leadership would come to a head at the worst possible moment.

Montezuma

The group topped up their stocks, bought some ammunition, and found Matt Hobbs a Colt .44 revolving rifle among the store's limited selection.

"Well, it's better than nothing, Matt," Moses chided, holding it over on him that he was better outfitted than the fancy Pinkerton.

Hobbs took the ribbing in stride, then feigned as if to grab Moses's rifle before laughing and slapping him on the back.

They had spent less than an hour in Covington and hoped to make Montezuma shortly after midday. Alternating between a healthy-paced walk and periods of a trot, they made good time, only needing to water the horses once on a cooler day than the last. All of them were quiet other than benign comments about their travel and surroundings, and they reached the bend in the river and railroad that Sheriff Taylor had told them would portend their arrival in Montezuma.

The small town of roughly five hundred people had a post office, a mercantile, and a few other clapboard buildings and tiny homes.

"Don't even see a building that has the law of any kind," Moses said.

The men slapped their reins around a hitching post in front of the post office and peered around at the signs above the scant few buildings. Elijah saw a rough-looking young man poke his head around from behind one of the buildings and quickly duck back in when he was seen. Elijah yelled out to the man, then headed for the building, Moses running after him.

Just as they reached the entrance to a small alley between two buildings, the man came barreling out on a horse, with Elijah and Moses having to jump out of the way. The other men quickly had their guns out, but the rider weaved around another building then was soon out of range, eventually turning toward Rockville.

"I don't suppose that was just some local fella worried we come with paper on him, was it?" Elijah stood and dusted himself off, looking to Moses to see if he was alright.

"Well, that rules out a surprise arrival in Rockville, I think." Hobbs beat his hat on his leg in disgust.

Marshal Foster shook his head and walked into the post office, re-emerging quickly and pointing toward the small mercantile store halfway down the main, and only, street. The heavy boots of five men on his wooden floor caused the man behind the counter to drop his feet off of it, and their badges and guns had him standing up quickly from his chair.

"What can I do for you gentlemen?"

"Old timer at the post office says you're the shopkeep *and* justice of the peace?" Marshal Foster stepped up to the desk as the other men looked around.

"Yessir, mostly a volunteer post, the latter is, bein' such a small town and all." He looked nervously at the door, where Talbot stood eyeing him.

Hobbs stepped up to the counter and asked, "What happens if the justice of the peace needs to attend to any business?"

"Well, I close up and see to it," the man said, sweating slightly. "Don't come up very often though."

"What about when folks show up with questions about Rockville?" Marshal Foster had changed the tone in his voice, apparently not liking the man's demeanor.

"Well," the man began, shifting his weight and scratching his head, "it usually depends what they're asking and what's in it for me."

"Maybe you didn't notice that man is the federal law," Talbot said. His voice turned the man's face white. "And that you are no real law at all."

The man gulped and saw that, satisfied there was nobody else in the building, Elijah and Moses had joined the crowd at the counter. "Listen, I get real nervous when folks talk about Rockville these days."

"I'd say," Moses said, pulling a handkerchief out of his pocket and handing it to the man. He wiped his brow and offered it back. Moses held up his hand, indicating for him to keep it.

"So, we get a fella spy us, then hightail it out of here toward Rockville, then you get all sweaty when we simply say the town's name," Marshal Foster said.

The man began mumbling, unable to find words, and Elijah lost his patience, knowing Ace would now have even more warning. "Dang it, man." He slammed a fist down on the counter. "There are two dead detectives up in Attica on a train that was robbed, bearing an awful lot of similarity to a bank robbery in Lafayette, and we're pretty sure we're going to find some answers in Rockville. We sure would like to know what those answers might look like."

Elijah stepped back and gave Marshal Foster a look—his feelings on stepping in where the marshal hadn't had gone from apologetic to necessary.

"Things been real strange in the county lately," the man began, "especially over there in Rockville. Some fella come in there—apparently grew up there—come home from the war suddenly in a bunch of money. There's some suspicious fires; he starts buying up the burnt-out properties and improving them and such . . ." He trailed off and looked at the men as if for approval. "Plus, now there's some kind of posse or vigilante group trying to take matters into their own hands. They hung a few fellers. People is scared."

"That's more like it," Hobbs said. "Keep it up."

Elijah stood back, pleased that his tactic had gotten the man talking.

"Listen, fellas, marshals, whatever you are. All I knows is anyone I'd think to be completely honest, or without money, has had a real hard go of it around here lately. Word makes its way around, and then when some rough lookin' fellas show up and tell you their boss wants to know if anyone is askin' about Rockville . . ." He stopped suddenly.

"You take their money," Talbot grumbled from the door.

"Mister, this store don't make a man rich."

The marshals all exchanged a look.

"Who was the kid on the horse riding off to see so quickly?" Hobbs asked the question casually, now that the man was talking.

"Mr. Tucker, I 'spect, or someone close to him . . ." The man flinched and trailed off.

Hobbs smiled. Elijah realized the Pinkerton had just been waiting for a chance to get the man to say a little too much. Elijah knew what to do on horseback with a gun, but he was learning a lot about investigating.

"What's his first name? How would we know him?" Elijah leaned in closely. "Mister, whatever trouble you think you could ever be in with Rockville and this Tucker only ends by helping us out."

The man sunk his head. "Frank Tucker, runs the Blue Union—the saloon, and the inn with a small tavern—"

"Can't believe a deserting, soldier murderer like him uses the name *Blue Union*," Elijah muttered.

The shopkeeper looked at Elijah with a raised eyebrow and continued. “If he ain’t glad handing government officials or business types or scarin’ them, he’s watching things at the saloon or the inn.”

Marshal Foster looked at Elijah, who nodded, and Foster rapped his knuckles on the counter.

“Now, that wasn’t so hard,” Hobbs said. He gave the man a condescending pat on the arm.

“We’re going to head over to that tree next to the river,” Marshal Foster said. He looked to the shopkeeper and then pointed out a window. “Going to have a bite to eat and water the horses. We’ll be watching this building while we do, and I trust we won’t see you heading anywhere before we’re finished.”

WITH THE HORSES WATERED and hobbled in the grassy shade, the men grabbed some of the small food items they’d bought in Covington and sat against the tree with their canteens, ensuring they were watching all directions.

Between bites, they discussed the pros and cons of riding into the town guns blazing, coming in peaceful and unannounced, peaceful and announced, and every other thing they could conceive.

“From the sounds of it,” Matt Hobbs spoke up, “the weight of the law isn’t going to mean much. That is to say, Tucker and his crew won’t care, and any sort of government or law in town has been scared into indifference.”

Foster looked at Moses.

Moses thought for a moment, then shrugged his shoulders. “I suppose it appears they’ll be ready for us and that we don’t know what sized army he’s got down the road.” He took a bite of a biscuit and seemed to think a bit more. "I like to think the three of us who done cavalry work can hold our own if we get them in the open, though."

"How about you, Talbot?" The marshal turned to him with a serious face. "If I've not shown it already, I greatly value your opinion, especially when it comes to how we'll interact with this town."

Talbot leaned his head back, then looked back at Marshal Foster. "I never had to deal with bank robbers, or clearly not train robbers," he said. He let that sink in momentarily as if to serve as a caveat. "Anytime I had to deal with findin' a fella in a town that maybe had some support or cover, I could always find someone ready to do the right thing."

Elijah realized that, aside from saving his life in Covington, this was precisely why they were lucky to have the old sheriff along. He knew what they were up against and that just focusing on difficulties wouldn't be helpful.

"Somebody, somewhere in that town, ain't on Tucker's payroll or on the take some other way. You never know who that is, and maybe they ain't even someone who can do nything' about it. They might be the person that can wake up the folks who could, though."

"I think Talbot's got it right, Marshal," Elijah said. He wanted to be the one who backed him up. "I vote we ride in 'n make no bones about who we are, and I 'spect that allows us to figure out who is who."

"And if that don't work?" Moses asked.

"I believe one way or another," the marshal said, "we aren't going to just ride in and arrest him without a scuffle." He stood and began to ready himself to leave.

The others hadn't even begun to stand when five riders with rifles, shotguns, and wearing revolvers came riding hard from the direction of Rockville over a rise to where the group of lawmen sat.

Elijah jumped to his feet, drawing his revolver as everyone else did the same.

Seeing the guns, the mounted strangers all drew as well, and their horses began circling and turning in a lather, the men spinning to keep their weapons trained on the marshal and his men.

"We heard a group of lawmen were on their way to look for Frank Tucker," their apparent leader shouted. "That you all?"

Elijah studied all the riders and realized one of them was the young man who'd almost trampled him and Moses not half an hour prior.

Vigilantes

The two groups held their weapons on each other as the few people out and about in Montezuma hurried indoors.

"Who are you?" the leader of the horsemen said quietly. Things were beginning to calm down.

"Solomon Foster, U.S. Marshal; my deputies; and Pinkerton Detective Matt Hobbs," he said. His demeanor was calm but assertive. "Identify yourselves."

The lead horseman eyed Foster and his men, then replaced his revolver in his holster, the other four riders following suit. "Name's George Adams," he said as he dismounted, keeping his hands in the air. He was a strong-looking, chisel-jawed man whom Elijah recognized was wearing parts of an army uniform. He looked the part of someone Elijah had made a corporal of on day one for just looking like the role of a soldier.

Marshal Foster lowered his weapon but did not holster it, and his men followed his lead. "We are, in fact, the law looking for Frank Tucker. State your business, sir."

Adams took a step closer to the group but continued to keep his hands held wide away from his body. Elijah didn't believe he saw any other weapons on the man; if so, they were concealed.

"We are concerned Rockville and Parke County citizens." He nodded to his group. "The last perhaps that care enough to, or have the fortitude for, doing something about him."

"Vigilantes, then." Marshal Foster had made a statement and was not asking a question.

"Or bounty hunters," Hobbs added, seemingly unpleased with the situation.

Adams leaned his head forward and studied Hobbs's Pinkerton badge. "Rich words, from a Pinkerton," he said but held his hands up before him when Hobbs made an angry face. "We are, I suppose, both of these things," he went on. He turned to Marshal Foster, "We're seeking the same thing you are. Did you give your arm in service to our great nation, Marshal Foster?"

The marshal holstered his weapon, turning to his men and gesturing to do the same. "I did, sir. At Champion Hill on the Vicksburg campaign. These two men to my left are brothers, Elijah and Moses Barber; they chased Price in Missouri." He nodded to Hobbs, "The Pinkerton was cavalry escort to General McClellan in the Army of the Potomac."

Adams nodded solemnly, then raised his chin in Talbot's direction.

"I was too old for all that," he said gravelly. "I've beat plenty of heads as a sheriff, though."

Elijah and Moses both turned and raised their eyebrows at Talbot.

Talbot just shrugged.

Elijah saw Moses staring intently at one of the riders.

"Iron Brigade, all of us," George Adams said. He waved his arm at his group. "Well, all but one. Antietam, Gettysburg, and the rest. All of that suffering, the loss of friends and family for your country, only to come home to a man like Tucker come back to be a crime boss with a grip on your home."

"Bounty jumper during the war, too," Elijah said with disdain. "I'm sure he ain't been telling of that."

Adams gave a curious look. "Well, I suppose that wouldn't surprise me none, either."

"You said all but one," Moses interjected. He was still staring intently at one of the riders.

Adams began to speak but was interrupted by the rider. "Yeah, I'm a woman," she said, removing her hat, long blonde hair falling.

"Dang, I knew it," Elijah said. He clapped his hands and had a smile on his face.

"That's Clara White," Adams said. "She grew up in the outdoors with her brothers who was both killed. She actually did some spying on aggressive copperheads down in the southern part of the state during the war."

Elijah raised an eyebrow.

"Well, I wore a dress for that," Clara quipped. "This gonna be a problem for you?" She stared back at Moses with a neutral expression on her face.

"Oh no, ma'am," Moses managed. His cheeks were turning red. "Name's Moses Barber; happy to meet you."

Elijah saw Talbot roll his eyes. He cleared his throat. "Back to the matter at hand," Elijah said. Adams's appeal and demeanor moved him. He began to wonder, however, if this wasn't some ploy by Tucker.

"We were on him for a bank robbery and just yesterday shot it out with him over a train robbery. We've only today learned of what you're dealing with here," Marshal Foster said, "but we're ready to put an end to it."

"Your news is news to us, but believable regardless. If you will allow us, we offer our services for whatever is to come," Adams said.

Marshal Foster looked at Hobbs, who gave his consent. "Go hobble your horses over with ours, and let's have ourselves a strategy session and get to know each other."

MARSHAL FOSTER SPOKE with George Adams privately for a bit, then asked that he might confer with his deputies and the Pinkerton agent. Returning to where his men were assembled, he asked, "What do you think?"

"You tell us, Marshal." Elijah just wanted him to lead for once.

"I sense all of your trepidation over whether this is some sort of trick by Tucker." The marshal saw all the men nodding. "You especially, Moses. I don't believe I've seen you take your hand off your holster."

"Not even when you were embarrassing yourself with the lady," Talbot said.

Moses quickly removed his hand and shook his head. "Sorry 'bout that." He turned and grimaced at Talbot, who winked back.

"I proposed," the marshal continued, "that we enter town ourselves, and asked if there wasn't a good spot we could rendezvous with them after we gather our first impressions. Adams says Tucker has roughly a dozen men doing rough work for him, in addition to himself and a number two named Charlie Wade who is always at his side. The Wade fella plays like he's his assistant and is the go-between with the thugs."

"Any word of the folks in town?" Talbot puffed on his pipe. "Sheriff, government types?" He was fishing for his theory about finding someone good.

"Said the sheriff isn't so much crooked as spineless. Upholds the law where it don't involve Tucker, and looks the other way to save his hide when it does. Government folks are just trying to grow the town, and business folks are either on that team or too scared to do anything about it. Said a whole lot of folks up and left town, and a lot of people who never thought they could own something got it on the cheap."

"So you're either on Tucker's team, or looking the other way for self-preservation sake," Elijah said. He was beginning to realize what they were up against.

"Appears the case," Marshal Foster said.

"Well, Marshal," Hobbs said, "I defer to you, but think we ride in acting like the only thing we know is to be checking the town, then link up with the vigilante bunch after."

"Anyone else just a little bit concerned about dealin' with these fellas?" Elijah wanted to be on record about it. "I don't trust that store owner turned justice of the peace any further than I could throw him, but he said there was a vigilante group scaring people."

"I don't want to be the sore thumb, and I know Eli don't either," Moses said, "but we dealt with this sort all the time in Missouri, and . . ." He trailed off and kicked at the dirt. "Best case, they don't show up when you need them; worst case, they turn on you."

Marshal Foster held his hand up, seeming to acknowledge the risk. "I figure we either aren't going to do this without some backup, which hopefully remains a surprise to Tucker that we use to our advantage..."

Elijah raised an eyebrow wanting to hear the alternative. "Or?"

"Or if it's a trap, I believe the fix would already be in, anyhow."

Elijah nodded and had to concede the point.

"Dictate the terms to them, Marshal," Talbot interjected. "If he don't push back on ya, that's about as good a feelin' as we're gonna get on how cooperative they'll be."

Marshal Foster looked to Adams and his group. "Mr. Adams," he shouted. "What's in this for you?"

Mr. Adams cocked his head, seeming to act insulted or as if it were apparent. "A return to normalcy for our county and the town," he said bluntly.

Good answer, thought Elijah.

"And nothing else?"

Adams looked at his group, then back at Marshal Foster. "I will not lie and say we don't also need to make a living of it in the process, what with honest work not currently able to be come by."

"I'd think him less honest if he didn't admit that," Talbot said.

"It's currently five hundred dollars for the capture of any man leading to information that brings about the killing or capture of, who we now know is, Frank Tucker. I believe you said there are a dozen of them. If you were to"—the marshal paused for effect—"ensure my deputies and I had these men pointed out to us, that would be mutually beneficial."

Adams nodded. "And Tucker himself?"

"Up to five thousand," the marshal announced. "The Pinkerton's job is to deliver him to me for justice, on behalf of the Pinkerton Agency, whom the bank hired. I believe Detective Hobbs would be generous, should your assistance prove helpful in that endeavor."

Marshal Foster looked at Talbot, who looked like he approved the negotiation.

"I'll be *half* generous," Hobbs said, shaking his head at the marshal.

"Plus, I expect the railroad will soon have an interest as well," Marshal Foster added.

George Adams briefly conferred with his group, then turned back to Marshal Foster. "Agreeable to us," he said, "with our trust in the word of a U.S. Marshal." He stepped closer to the group and added, "With my assurance, that the removal of Frank Tucker is our primary objective."

"Let us know where we'll find you then," Marshal Foster said, signaling his group to mount up. "And when next you see Detective Hobbs here"—he gestured at the Pinkerton—"please hide your recognition if he seems to be in the company of Tucker or Wade."

Hobbs cocked his head at Marshal Foster as he mounted his horse.

"Does your employer not pride itself on its often-undercover nature?" Marshal Foster asked.

Hobbs laughed, and the two headed off together.

Elijah grabbed Moses and approached George Adams as men mounted up around them. He briefly summarized their past interactions with Tucker. "Did you have occasion to coordinate well with the cavalry in the Iron Brigade, Mr. Adams?"

Adams smiled a broad grin. "Indeed, I did, Mr. Barber. Most especially at Gettysburg. Please call me George," he said, offering his hand to each brother.

"Elijah, and Moses," Elijah offered, as they each accepted his hand. "If the papers had it right, George," Elijah said, "the cavalry hung on in a tight spot until the infantry showed up to save their bacon. Is that your recollection?"

"It is, indeed, Elijah," George said with a smile.

"Well, George"—Elijah looked at Moses and then back at the former infantryman—"I 'spect that may well be called for again."

ROCKVILLE

While Matt Hobbs rode into town, without his Pinkerton badge, from the west, George Adams and his group led Marshal Foster and his men wide to the south, then back toward town from the east. Seeing where the vigilantes made camp, the marshals then headed for town. Elijah took in the modest-sized town and its mostly clapboard buildings. The main thoroughfare was lined with businesses and offices, and a few homes sat along some small side roads. The inn and tavern were in the town center, with the Blue Union saloon farther down to the west.

Hitching their horses to a post near the edge of town, the group saw a couple of broad-shouldered men in elegant clothes that didn't match their unrefined attitudes approaching them.

"What's your business here?" one of them said.

Marshal Foster removed his saddlebag and threw it over his shoulder as Elijah and Moses did the same with a close eye on the encounter. "Do you need an appointment to stop in this town?" the marshal asked.

The man shifted his jaw back and forth, then spit tobacco at Marshal Foster's feet. His partner was locked in a staring contest with Elijah.

"Nice rifles you got there," the staring man said, looking at Elijah.

"I seen your faces," Moses roared, "and I better see those rifles when I come back to my horse." He stared at the men intently. "Or else I know who to get 'em back from."

The men laughed and took a few steps back, then turned and walked away.

"Good job on the low profile, Mo," Elijah said. "You think they noticed our badges?"

"I'm sure they did," replied the marshal.

"They steal my darn rifle, Marshal, and there won't be anything low profile about my reaction," Moses said.

Marshal Foster just shook his head and began walking up the main street. "Remember, we're not hiding who we are but not making a big scene," he said. "Make some inquiries, make it seem like we're grasping at straws, and we meet in front of the inn at six." He pulled out his pocket watch and examined it, "That's when Hobbs said he would head downstairs to the tavern for dinner."

They passed a grocer, and Elijah saw a young boy looking out at them from the window. Elijah smiled, and the boy smiled back and waved before being pulled from the window by a woman.

"I'll talk to the sheriff and see if he's on the take, and you three see about confirming what we've heard about Tucker," the marshal said. He then headed toward the courthouse and adjacent building labeled *Parke County Sheriff*.

Elijah saw the boy re-emerge at the shop window and smiled at him again. He caught the end of Moses and Talbot saying where they were headed and began walking toward the grocery shop door.

A BELL JINGLED above the door as he opened it. Stepping inside, he did not immediately see the boy, so he examined the goods. The store was orderly and well-kept, but he noticed it didn't seem to carry as much stock as it was laid out for.

The boy suddenly appeared almost under his feet, and Elijah yelped in surprise. "Hello, young man."

"Are you some kinda law or something?" The boy was wide-eyed, alternating between Elijah's revolver and badge.

A woman emerged from behind the counter when she heard Elijah's yelp and saw the boy standing almost on top of him.

"John!" she exclaimed. "Manners."

The boy stepped away and hung his head.

"Oh, that's alright, ma'am," Elijah said. He noticed the woman appeared to be the proprietor, and nobody else was in the store. He thought that she was about his age, more or less, and found himself trying to decide whether it was a shade of light brown or red to her hair. She wore a blue and white gingham skirt, a white blouse, and a dark blue shawl. It all looked homespun but neatly so. He shocked himself to realize he was spending time admiring her beauty, even if she looked tired and troubled.

"I'm very sorry, Mr. . . ." she trailed off.

"Barber. U.S. Deputy Marshal."

"Well, yes, Deputy Barber, if that's how to call you. My John here is too curious for his own good sometimes and forgets how to act."

"My friends call me Johnny!" the boy exclaimed. He appeared to be over his scolding.

Elijah knelt at the boy's level. "Well, my friends call me Eli, Johnny."

The boy smiled and looked up at his mother as if for permission. She rolled her eyes, then relented.

"Eli, are you really a deputy marshal?" His eyes were wide.

Elijah turned the badge on the side of his chest toward the boy. "That's what it says right there."

"Wow!"

Elijah stood and looked at the woman as if he wished to speak without the boy present.

"John, will you please go in the back and check that none of the newly arrived produce is bad?"

He made a face as if to protest, but Elijah's wink and nod sent him running off.

"Elijah Barber, if I may be more formal ma'am," Elijah extended his hand. "Is John your boy?"

"Mary Adams," she said. She lightly accepted his hand and turned back toward the counter at the back of the store. "He is."

Elijah followed her. "I've only just arrived in town," he said. He was looking around to see who else, if anyone, was around. "Are you a relation to a Mr. George Adams?" He wondered if he shouldn't be revealing his association but hoped for the best.

"My brother-in-law," she said quietly. Before Elijah could inquire further, she continued. "My husband died at Gettysburg." She stopped moving and looked up at Elijah with a hand on her hip. "George looks after us," she said, "when he's actually around."

Elijah, who was suddenly horrified to realize he had left his hat on the whole time, removed it and held it before him. "I'm very sorry for your loss, ma'am."

"Did you fight too, Mr. Barber?" She had an exasperated look on her face.

"I did, ma'am. From Illinois, I served mostly in Missouri in the cavalry."

"I run a store alone in this town because of men with guns, that is now run by men with guns. So I suppose new men with guns are here to save me?"

Elijah rubbed his chin as he considered how to answer this.

"That you have enough sense to not try and justify all that is an improvement, Mr. Barber." She smiled faintly.

"Well, ma'am," Elijah began, "since you have broached it, I am indeed here with other men hoping to do something about your town's situation." He explained what they had learned over the last few days, and she confirmed everything they had put together.

"As you can see, my store has struggled greatly since my husband left, and is only worse since I refuse to play nice with Mr. Tucker. He is currently building an addition to his saloon I'm told will be a mercantile that fully puts me out of business." She put her hands on the counter and stared out the window momentarily. "I suppose he decided outright running a war widow off wouldn't help his case, but I fear I've pushed back long enough that he'll soon no longer care."

Elijah frowned. "I wish I could tell you we could fix it right this second, ma'am, but we don't yet have a warrant."

"Even though you have almost no doubt of what he has done?"

"That's correct, ma'am."

She shook her head. "Elijah, if I can call you that—"

"Please," he interjected.

"My husband was a good man, not as present a father as he maybe should have been in his brief opportunity to have been one, but a good man. All my boy knows in life, however, is that a good man went to war and died. His uncle, a good man, was run out of town for trying to do the right thing, albeit with some oftentimes questionable tactics. Now, a very bad man reaps the rewards that I am trying to raise my son to see are for a good and honest man . . . or woman . . . to have."

Elijah just looked at her, letting her see he was listening intently.

"Are you a good man, Elijah?"

Elijah ran his hand through his hair and looked everywhere but at Mary Adams. "I like to think so, Mrs. Adams." He returned her gaze. "I worshiped my pa, then worked my tail off to support my ma when he died. I worshiped the man who stepped into his place, learned the word of God from all of them, looked out for my brother . . ." He paused, wiping at his eyes. "Had a brother to take care of, and then we went to war too."

She stepped from behind the desk and stood in front of him.

"I done things in the war, ma'am, that make me hate violence more than about anything in the world. I know I pressed men harder than I should." His voice got quiet. "I know I was often more violent than maybe called for. But I like to think I did it for the right reasons. I believed in what we were fightin' for, but mostly I was just trying to take care of my brother and the other men."

"Be a good man for this town then, please. I don't need a man to help me run this store, but . . ." She trailed off. "Whether I like it or not, it does appear I need one to give me the chance to do so."

"I understand." He toed at the dusty floor with his boot. "I been learnin' a thing or two about how some things are, whether I like 'em or not."

"Whatever the outcome is, give me somebody to tell my boy to look at." She looked back to see Johnny peering through the curtain leading to the stock room. "Because right now, that man doesn't exist in this town."

Dinner and a Show

Matt Hobbs sat at a table alone in the simply named Rockville Inn and Tavern, finishing the last of his meal. After conferring with the group on where they would be, he had put on his clean change of clothes and checked into the inn bearing a dignified but edgy persona.

His arrival had been uneventful, but after coming down from his room to eat, he had multiple sets of eyes on him.

"Anything else for you, sir?" The waiter gathered Hobbs's plates. "We've got some fresh cobbler."

Hobbs removed a cigar from his coat pocket and waved his hand dismissively. "Just a glass of brandy to go with the cigar."

"Right away, sir."

Hobbs forcefully grabbed the man's arm, as if it were nothing. "I'd also like to know where I could find Mr. Tucker this evening."

The waiter gulped hard, and when Hobbs let go of his arm, he snatched it back. "I'll be right back with that brandy, mister."

Across the street, Elijah leaned against a hitching post, looking into the tavern's dining room and watching the scene unfold. Moses sat on a bench just outside, his hat pulled low, and Talbot and Marshal Foster also stood nearby, forming a diamond in front of the building.

Elijah lit his pipe and began to puff, then nodded to the other three men.

The waiter had re-emerged with the glass of brandy and a well-dressed man who looked as if he had won and lost an equal number of fights. His nose was disfigured, and he had some scars, but he somehow managed to still look refined. The waiter set the brandy down and quickly walked away before Hobbs could finish a puff of his cigar and call after him with a thank you.

"Won't you sit?" Hobbs gestured to the chair across from him and offered a cigar, which Charlie Wade declined.

"Do you often invite strangers to your table, mister . . ."

"Hobbs," he replied. He drank half the glass of brandy then offered his hand. "Matt Hobbs."

Wade hesitantly accepted it, looking around the room.

So far, so good, Elijah thought, watching through the window.

"I would have been suspicious," Hobbs continued, "had I not received a visit from a man such as yourself after my inquiry." He finished the brandy.

"Man such as myself?" Wade raised an eyebrow.

"Believe me, this is not an insult," Hobbs said. He tapped the ashes from his cigar into the empty brandy glass with his left hand. "I didn't catch your name, sir."

"I didn't give it," Wade replied. "What was your inquiry?"

"I would like an audience with Mr. Tucker," Hobbs replied. He fixed a stare at the man across the table from him.

"And say *a man such as myself* could arrange that meeting. Why would I do that?"

"Mr. Tucker's return from service to his country, followed by such a capable building up of his own personal wealth, and his hometown along with it, is of great interest to me. I can only assume he would like to see Rockville have a role in the Indianapolis to St. Louis railroad. Everyone needs a profession in life, and mine is helping men like him protect themselves and what they have"—he paused for effect—"and find ways to grow it."

"You some kind of law? And what would you know 'bout Mr. Tucker's wealth and means?" There was the faint clicking noise of a hammer cocking under the table.

"I am to assume," Hobbs said, "that you know I've also have a gun held on you, yes?"

The man nodded. He then nodded to a man in the corner with his hand on his hip and to the tapper inside the cage bar, who Hobbs realized likely had a long gun of some sort.

"I am very much not the law; quite the opposite, sir. As for how exactly he accumulates what he does, I am a smart enough man to be somewhat informed as to it, and even smarter to not speak of it."

Wade gave a slight grin.

"So, you're in the business of helping influential men like Mr. Tucker? What bonafides do you have to such a profession?"

Hobbs puffed on his cigar. "Well, I suppose formally you would call my law degree from New York, of which I originally hail, a professional bonafide. My less formal qualifications are more of the"—he twirled the cigar in the air—"a nature that needs to be demonstrated." He looked around the room, then placed his right hand on the table. "Might we do this without the weapons?"

The man placed his hands on the table, then nodded to the other men. "Continue, then."

"For example," Hobbs said, "were you aware of the U.S. Marshals walking about your town?"

Wade looked up at the door with a raised eyebrow. "Mighta heard something of the sort. Haven't seen it myself yet, though. If they are here, as you say, they followed you, and I ought to replace that gun under the table."

"Quite the opposite, sir." Hobbs smashed the butt of his cigar on the table and wiped the ashes to the floorboards. "I followed them from Attica, just yesterday. Quite a huff they were in about something with a train."

"How did you know—"

Hobbs cut him off while dropping the dignified tone and fixing a stare on Wade. "The boy and his friend from the train station are no longer a concern." He sat back, straightened his jacket, and resumed in his dignified voice, "I should hope the fact that I maintain *some* decorum and did not bring proof of such will not be held against me."

Wade raised his chin and an eyebrow, then stood and offered his hand. "Charlie Wade, Mr. Hobbs."

"A pleasure," Hobbs replied, accepting his hand.

"Let's go somewhere more private."

"The saloon?" Hobbs asked. He stood as well.

"You'll find out when we get there," Wade said. He eyed Hobbs. "You ain't what you say you are, and I'll kill ya myself."

Hobbs held his hands before him with a smile, then put his hat on.

Elijah saw the men preparing to exit the inn and quickly nodded to Moses. Hobbs engaged the man in small talk and gave a discreet nod to Moses. When the two passed him, Moses tapped his nose at Elijah, who returned the gesture, pushed himself off the hitching post, and began following Wade and Hobbs.

The two men were walking down the middle of the street, and Elijah and Marshal Foster were now doing the same, following closely behind. Moses and Talbot lingered along the building fronts on either side of the thoroughfare. Hobbs had argued he should be allowed to be taken to Tucker, if possible, but Marshal Foster had been against it.

Marshal Foster called out loudly when they were almost in front of the saloon. "Excuse me, sir."

Hobbs waited for Wade to stop walking, then did the same. Wade turned and eyed Foster first. Elijah thought he detected a hint of recognition in Wade's eyes. "Talkin' to me?" he said.

"I am," Marshal Foster said, displaying his badge.

Elijah noticed the few people out and about were moving off the street. A man with a horse and wagon quickly sped past them, not wanting to be involved in whatever was happening. Elijah realized people around here were used to getting out of the way.

Hobbs began to move away from Wade, who eyed him scornfully. Charlie Wade casually pulled his coat away from his holster, and Elijah did the same.

"What can I do for the one-armed marshal?" Charlie Wade asked.

Hobbs walked past Marshal Foster, whispering the man's name to him, then returning to the tavern.

"My name is U.S. Marshal Solomon Foster, Mr. Wade."

Elijah saw Wade contort his face.

"You and your boss have been busy men," Marshal Foster said. "A bank in Lafayette, a train in Attica."

Talbot saw a man near him on the wood-planked sidewalk begin to reach for a revolver and calmly put his own in the man's back. "That would be the last mistake you ever make, son," he whispered in his gravelly voice. The man removed his hand from his holster and backed away to lean on a building.

Elijah looked at Moses, then Talbot, and saw that they were tallying up anyone they thought to be a hired gun on the street.

"No idea what you're speaking of, Marshal." Wade spat into the dirt street and looked around. "Heard somethin' about all that, but sounds like the men all had bags over their heads. Would be awfully hard to figure who it was. As to who you say my boss is"—he nodded at the inn, then over at the Blue Union—"he owns two successful businesses and is the benefactor of many others in this town."

"Talk all you want, Wade," Elijah interjected. "You think we can't recognize voices, statures"—he paused to emphasize the next point—"eccentric behaviors and leave-behinds at the scenes of these crimes?"

Wade tried to maintain his face of defiance, but Elijah wondered if he didn't see a brief reaction on Wade's face. Perhaps one that had often said *I told you to knock it off with the playing cards.*

"Tucker wants to be famous, Mr. Wade." Foster took a couple of steps closer as he talked. "Maybe for being wealthy, but not for doing it as a legitimate business owner. It's got him caught, and that means it's got you caught, too."

Wade looked from Marshal Foster to Elijah and put his hand on his revolver, the deputies doing the same. Every window on the street had faces, and those who remained on the street had backed away as far as possible.

A door opened on the second-floor deck of the saloon, and a man appeared at the railing.

"Marshal, I'm so glad to see you," he yelled. The man had a look of appreciation on his face.

Marshal Foster tilted his head slightly and eyed Elijah, who nodded at him. "All yours," the marshal whispered.

"Hello, Frank," Elijah yelled up to the balcony.

Having not yet talked to Wade about the arrival of these men in town, he was no doubt somewhat surprised at what was unfolding, at least that it had come about this quickly. However, he did not show it and stood with both hands pressed against the balcony as if he was presiding over some official forum.

"Someone fetch the sheriff," Tucker said. "Marshal, I trust you'll be able to make use of the sheriff's assistance in helping us with a problem we are having." He waited to see one of the armed men on the side of the street hustle off toward the sheriff's office. The assembled crowd saw Tucker poke his head back into the building and then return.

A moment later, there was a scuffle at the saloon's front door, and two men dragged another between them. The man was bloodied, his clothes torn, and he struggled mightily. They brought him to the street, throwing him down in the dirt and putting guns on him.

The man raised his head slowly, and Elijah recognized the face of George Adams. From the corner of his eye, Elijah saw the sheriff approaching him with a look of resignation.

"We've had an awful problem with vigilantes, Marshal," Tucker called out again. "This one has been leading a gang seeing fit to take the law into their own hands. Hung two of my employees for supposed crimes they received no trial for. We have caught him, however, and turn him over to you, Sheriff. I trust you can hold him while catching up the marshal and his deputies on his transgressions. I know ruffians attempting to enforce justice outside of the law is of much interest to a lawman like yourself."

Whatever else was going to transpire, Marshal Foster seemingly did not want a shootout at this moment and pulled his hand away from his revolver, motioning for everyone else to do the same.

"Your arrival is most opportune indeed, Marshal," Tucker continued. "I'm sure you're quite the busy man, though; plenty of work to do around the state. *Plenty of crimes you can actually prove,*" he said with emphasis. Tucker now motioned for all of his men to relax as well.

"That's how it is then, Frank?" Marshal Foster looked at Adams, then up at Tucker.

"I've caught you before and there won't be a second chance for escape," Elijah called up to him.

"I have no idea what you mean, deputy," Tucker said. "I expect that not to be the case, however." He looked at Marshal Foster. "You can take him with you, or we can facilitate the hanging right here. Either way, we'll *be sure* to see you on your way tomorrow." Nobody listening to Tucker's words and tone was confused about his meaning. The marshals would be out of the way tomorrow, one way or another.

The sheriff had the two thugs begin walking George Adams toward his office, the lawman unable to meet Marshal Foster and Elijah's eyes as they glared at him. Tucker retreated into the building, and Wade waved with a smile as he walked toward the saloon.

"We'll talk in camp," Marshal Foster said, his face stern as he turned and began walking back through town to his horse.

"Be right behind you," Elijah said, then walked toward Moses. "How many?"

"At least a dozen, Eli," Moses replied.

Talbot joined them, hearing their conversation. "Plus, the two dragging Adams around, and whoever is in the saloon or anywhere else." He took another look around and bit his lip. "Few of 'em look green, but most look like they can handle themselves."

"Talbot's right. Most of 'em ain't parlor soldiers." Moses shook his head. "This ain't some faraway territory out west," he said. "What in God's name is goin' on 'round here?"

"Don't take much for a man like him to strong arm an emerging town like this, no matter where you are," Talbot said. "'Specially if it's benefittin' plenty'a folks."

"Marshal wants to talk back in our camp," Elijah said. "I'll be right behind you. Woman that runs the grocery is a widow to Adams's brother. Gonna stop in and let her know the lay of things."

THE STORE WAS CLOSED, and Elijah assumed Mary Adams and her son were in the back living quarters he had spied on his earlier visit. He knocked softly, then after no answer, a bit more aggressively. He heard a shuffling, then saw a shadow in the window. Mary opened the door holding a candle, the bell giving its jingle into the night.

"I'm awfully sorry to call this late, Mrs. Adams," Elijah said with his hat in his hands. "I've got news of your brother-in-law."

She brought her hand to her mouth and went wide-eyed.

"Oh, no; he's alive," Elijah said. "May I . . ." He paused, concerned about the appearance of coming in at the late hour but worried about standing in the street any longer.

Seeming to sense all of this, Mary opened the door fully. "Of course."

Elijah stepped inside. "Is the boy asleep?"

She nodded.

"Tucker has caught up George somehow and turned him over to the sheriff. He knows why we're here but is playing his hand that he has deniability and making a show of acting like we were here for the vigilantes." Elijah saw her look of concern. "He's bloodied up pretty good but seems to be alright otherwise."

She hung her head. "And what next from the U.S. Marshals then?"

"We're about to go discuss that. If it were up to me, we'd go to war with him in the morning, as I fear what happens to this town, or him disappearing for good, if we don't."

Mary seemed to consider all this and stared into his eyes. "You know war and fighting doesn't always fix things, Deputy Barber."

Elijah began to open his mouth to reply, but she interrupted. "Sometimes it is the only course, though." She paused momentarily before continuing, "For good men to press the violence in the short term, that it may end in the long term."

"I understand," Elijah said. He stood awkwardly for a moment; then she broke the silence.

"Is there a Mrs. Barber that is somewhere worrying about you?"

Elijah shook his head. "No ma'am. I reckon there was a prospective one back in Danville, but I'm not a wise man in those affairs." He smiled and noticed that she did, too. "I suppose she's worrying nonetheless."

"Is there anything I can do for you all now?" Mary asked. "Aside from doing some worrying for you?"

Elijah chuckled. "If you have occasion in the morning to pass the word of what is going on . . ." He paused. "I can't expect people to fight, but to just stand for us in one way or another will be of use." He put his hat back on his head. "I like to think there's good people here, even if they've been acting in self-preservation."

She nodded, and Elijah began to move to the door.

"You were too hard on yourself earlier," she said.

"Pardon?" He looked back, confused.

"You put too many restrictions on yourself when I asked if you were a good man."

Elijah's face felt hot. He had long ago started refusing any compliments he received. "Thank you," he said. He opened the door and stepped outside. "Good night, Mrs. Adams."

"Good night, Deputy Barber."

Elijah heard the bell jingle and the door close behind him. He saw Marshal Foster, Moses, and Talbot unwrapping the reins of their horses off to his right. He began to move in their direction, looking back down the street before doing so. He saw the sheriff exiting his office with a lantern and thought he noticed a couple of Tucker's thugs standing out front.

"Elijah," Marshal Foster called after him. Elijah was already walking diagonally across the street, however. He was moving straight toward the sheriff with what Moses had once called his "command stare."

"Is it fear, then, or cowardice?" Elijah got so close to the sheriff that the man had to turn his face away as he backed up a step.

"What are you talking about?" Sheriff Lawrence Miller was trying to keep his voice low, and Elijah saw him eyeing the thugs out of the corner of his eye, menacing grins on their faces.

Marshal Foster and his two deputies had made their way to Elijah, and Moses put a hand on Elijah's shoulder, causing Elijah to jerk.

"Not right now, brother," Moses said.

Elijah shook him off and fixed a long stare on the sheriff, who looked like he wanted to crawl into the ground. "Go on home, then, I guess," Elijah said to the sheriff. "Choose security over doing the right thing."

The sheriff hung his head, grabbed his horse's reins, and began walking away.

"Alright, let's go," Marshal Foster said.

Elijah turned briefly as if to acknowledge him but then looked back to the thugs. Their devilish grins made him want to drop them both where they stood. "You two," he began. He took a step toward them, pointing a menacing finger. "You have hitched your wagon to a devilish horse, and your time is fixin' to be up."

One of them raised his hands in mock-surrender, and the other just stared back.

"Eli!" Talbot's voice sounded fatherly, his name alone conveying all the meaning.

Elijah spun on his boot heel, ignoring the marshal and deputies as he walked past them toward Bear. He was tired. He was tired of being put in positions to help people and feeling he had failed. He was tired of Marshal Foster never being ready to act. He wasn't going to let it happen again.

Camp Feud

"Count me not at all surprised they're gone," Talbot said. He was occupying himself over the fire with a pot of coffee. "Everyone talks a big game until things get tough."

The group had returned to camp to find the vigilante group gone, apparently having received word of the fate of their leader. Fearing being out in the wide open, they'd established camp inside a covered bridge, with their fire and horses just outside.

"Word travels fast in this town," Hobbs replied. He was going through his saddlebags. "Went back to the inn to say I wouldn't be staying after all, and the clerk got real twitchy. Told me I'd better hurry up, get my things, and get out of there."

Moses stepped near the small fire and accepted Talbot's coffee before sitting on a stump. "Now what?"

"Well," Marshal Foster began, "I do figure we owe it to George Adams to go get him out in the morning. He's in this fix on account of us."

"Maybe he'll go round his group back up," Moses offered.

Talbot finished his coffee and shook his head. "Or hightail it on out of here." He got out his pipe and began packing it. "Or it's like we feared, and they've turned against us."

"Not helpful, Talbot," Moses said.

"They won't just let us ask for him to be released and walk out as a free-looking man," Marshal Foster said. "Best case scenario: we have to make him look a prisoner."

Elijah had been leaning against a tree outside the circle of men at the fire. "Well, aren't we just as bad as that worthless sheriff," he muttered loud enough to be heard.

"Should we talk now about how worthless your interaction with the sheriff back in town was?" Marshal Foster didn't even turn to look at Elijah as he spoke.

Elijah stomped into the center of the group and stood next to the fire. "What in God's name are we even doing here if we are going to just let Tucker walk all over this town, get away with murder, with bank and train robbing?"

Marshal Foster stood and stepped to Elijah. "What would you have me do, Elijah?"

"Your job!"

"Alright, alright," Talbot said. Moses and Hobbs had stepped between the men, and each man held up a hand indicating the confrontation had passed.

Marshal Foster looked up, and where Elijah expected a look of anger, he saw one of resignation. "He holds all the cards, Elijah."

Elijah scrunched his face at the reference, his agitation growing. He looked around the assembled group, seeking backup, but the men were silent. He poured a cup of coffee and sat on the ground. He took a drink, then began picking out blades of grass and tossing them. "You were right, Talbot."

Talbot looked up at him with a raised eyebrow.

"This was a fool's errand."

Talbot looked back at him with a look Elijah had never seen from him. His eyes seemed to convey that he wasn't saying *I told you so* or anything like that. Talbot's face seemed to express a sadness that he couldn't do more to help him. Elijah's thoughts were interrupted by Hobbs.

"What about wiring for some help? I could send for more Pinkertons?"

Marshal Foster shook his head. "If they've got a telegraph office, I'll wager all I've got that he has someone monitoring all the wire traffic in and out. The message might not even get sent, and even if it does, he'll just assemble even more of an army during the wait."

"Then we do something about it tomorrow when they aren't expecting it," Elijah said. He jumped to his feet and looked around at the men once again.

"Elijah, no," the marshal replied.

Elijah began to walk off, then stopped and turned at the edge of their tiny circle. "Is that what you did moving down the Mississippi with Grant? Now I wasn't there, but from what I remember reading, you all ran into one obstacle after another but just kept your head down and eventually won out." Elijah stared at him for a moment wanting a response, but getting none, marched to the edge of the bridge and leaned against it. He stood in the shadows, glaring at the fire.

For a minute, the only sound was the crackling of the fire and the chirp of the summer night's crickets.

"I didn't fight one bit in the war; I was worthless." Marshal Foster's sudden confession broke the silence.

The men all looked up, and Elijah pushed himself away from the bridge.

Marshal Foster was staring at the ground, then looked up suddenly, pain in his eyes. "They made me a colonel because I had the money and family ties to get a regiment together. Had hardly ever fired a weapon or done anything violent or dangerous or backbreaking a day in my life. I was a liability. My lieutenant colonel ran the regiment, and I always had a reason to be away at a meeting. Men didn't respect me; I cowered away in battle."

The men all shifted uncomfortably, and Elijah returned to the circle.

"At Champion Hill, my lieutenant colonel got badly wounded early on, and we had a new brigade commander that I guess wasn't aware of the unspoken rule to not actually have Colonel Foster do anything." He chuckled awkwardly at this memory. "He sent me forward with my men, and I rode around like an idiot until the grapeshot tore through my arm. I was a phony for that job, and a phony for this one."

The men were silent, and Elijah eventually sat beside him.

Elijah put a hand on Marshal Foster's shoulder. He wanted to tell him that all that seemed a far more normal human reaction to the violence of that war than riding into it unafraid, that he shouldn't have felt the need to misrepresent himself just because he and Moses had been fighters, that he was sorry for bombarding him with his poor attitude. Instead, he just patted his shoulder, hoping the marshal understood.

The marshal looked up and made eye contact with his deputies. "If you men will have it, I'll hang onto the legal authority, but I suggest we make Elijah our leader if we have to fight this out."

The group was silent again, all of them a bit unsure of the situation.

"Are you with me on that at least?" the marshal asked.

"Yessir," Moses said. He gave Elijah a proud look.

Hobbs nodded. "No offense, Marshal, but I'm more used to taking cavalry commands, anyhow."

Marshal Foster gave a small smile and looked at Talbot. "That OK with you?"

Talbot stood and poured out the dregs of his coffee, puffing on his pipe. "Well, I can't say I'm thrilled at the prospect of taking commands from a boy I practically raised." He walked to where Elijah stood and gave him a look of approval—one Elijah had spent years seeking. "I think it's what ought to happen, though." He turned to the marshal. "This by the book?"

Marshal Foster threw up his hands. "I think we threw the book out a long time ago on this case."

Talbot turned back to Elijah and stuck out his hand. Elijah accepted and shook it vigorously, a small tear appearing in the corner of his eye.

"Don't you even dare, boy," Talbot said. He turned to the rest of the group. "Anyone have something stronger than coffee, before we go sharing any more feelings?"

Moses jumped up with a smile and dug in his saddlebags, producing a bottle. "I'd been saving it for a happy outcome, but I reckon we could all use it."

Elijah laughed, and Talbot slapped him on the back. However, when they heard the nicker of a horse and hooves on the bridge, along with two approaching lanterns, the bottle was forgotten, and they all reached for their guns.

Fire

"Hello the marshal camp," a voice called. "Can we come in?" It was Sheriff Miller.

"Well, I'll be," Elijah said. He holstered his weapon, and the other men did the same.

Marshal Foster looked at Elijah with a raised eyebrow. "Seems your dressing down had an effect after all."

The group watched as Sheriff Miller rode into view and dismounted, George Adams appearing on the other horse. He was moving gingerly, but Elijah didn't think he observed any lasting injury in the light of the lanterns and fire.

There were handshakes and greetings as the deputies guided Adams to the fire, and Moses offered the bottle around to any who wanted a pull.

"You had every right to say what you did back in town earlier." The sheriff looked to each man in the group, stopping at Elijah. "I still don't deserve much praise, though. Young deputy I got is a good man. Told Tucker's crew he was watching the back of the office, but he's better than that. I got to finally feeling sorry for myself at home and come back to find him leading Adams out the back of the building."

Talbot shot a look at Marshal Foster. "Told you there's always someone."

Elijah poured a cup of coffee each for Adams and the sheriff, then sat down facing them with his chin on his fist. "Go on then, sheriff."

"Said he was fixin' to let him go, but I told him I didn't want him taking that risk to lead him out of town." He took a drink of his coffee. "Told George here that I thought we owed it to you to pay a visit, and he said he knew where you'd be."

"As you can see," Elijah said, "the rest of your friends abandoned us when they heard you got rolled up."

George Adams frowned and looked at Elijah. "Yeah, I don't much care for it either," he said. "I had big thoughts of what we could accomplish, but most of them folks have families and when things started getting real . . ." He trailed off, but his point was made.

"Any chance you can get them back?" Moses asked.

"I can sure try," Adams said.

"Need a man? Some food?" Marshal Foster asked.

Adams shook his head and finished his coffee as he rose. "Deputy fed me before he sprung me. I best go alone." He looked up at the bright moonlight of the evening.

Elijah shook the sheriff's hand, then offered it to George Adams, who accepted it. "We'll wait for you and any backup you can bring before we move. We haven't thought it all the way through yet, but I expect our best bet is if any kind of skirmish starts in town, to ride hard this way and hopefully lead them into an ambush from you."

Adams looked to Marshal Foster for approval, but the marshal only pointed back at Elijah. "Alright then," Adam said.

"Come find us one way or another. Regardless of what you round up, and we'll go from there."

Adams shook the hands of the others and mounted his horse. With a yell and a kick, he was off into the night.

"How about you, Sheriff?" Elijah gave the man his command stare again but adopted a softer tone than earlier. "Are you with us?"

"Reckon I prefer it didn't come to needing me," he said, "but I sure won't stand in your way or interfere."

Elijah caught Moses and Talbot's eyes and gave a disappointed look that they returned. Marshal Foster looked away and ran his hand through his hair. However, Elijah considered it an improvement and decided not to press the issue. "Much obliged," he said.

"We best get what rest we can," Marshal Foster said. He walked to his horse and began his one-handed effort to undo his bedroll.

"Maybe don't ride straight back into town from here," Elijah offered. He watched the sheriff mount up, fighting a strong desire to demand more out of him.

The sheriff touched the brim of his hat, then turned his horse and made off in a wide arc to return to town.

They all watched him until the vast night sky swallowed him up, then turned back to one another.

"We'll be lucky if he doesn't lock himself in his office tomorrow, if he even leaves home," Talbot said.

The men all murmured in agreement.

"How 'bout Adams?" Moses turned toward where he had ridden off, then back to the group. "Think we see him again?"

"Slightly better odds," Talbot said. "I got little hope for him bringing a posse, though."

"Alright," said Elijah. "Let's get a couple hours rest, and we'll see what the morning holds." He wanted to drink more coffee and stay up all night, making a plan. However, the effort would be useless until he knew what kind of force he commanded. "We'll plan once we know what we're working with."

WANTING TO BE READY at a moment's notice, the group all laid down with their boots on. They had strung a rope between trees just outside the bridge and tied the horses with their saddles on.

Elijah lay awake for a long time, listening to the echo of the stream and the night's insects inside the bridge. There was a cool breeze blowing through, and had it not been for the situation, he would have enjoyed the setting.

His mind was full of scenarios the next day could bring, but he quickly dismissed them all as he realized he had no real idea. Given the wartime experience of himself, Moses, and Hobbs, he thought they could take advantage if Adams brought other former soldiers to bear. He tossed and turned, trying to get comfortable, wondering if Tucker thought they'd avoid an outnumbered fight. Privately, he just wished Tucker would give him an excuse to gun him down. He eventually fell asleep at some point, waking up to Talbot shaking him.

"Eli, I think we got trouble," Talbot said.

Elijah shook the sleep from his brain and looked around the camp. The others were now stirring. They realized George Adams had never returned. The early morning was still dark, with the faintest beginning of light in the eastern sky leaking onto the bridge. Then Elijah smelled it, far more smoke than any cooking fire would produce.

Talbot nodded, a frown on his face, and pointed to the edge of the town nearest them. Elijah sat up and saw the orange glow of what must have been a building on fire.

"That son of a . . ." Elijah was up and pulling on his hat as he approached Bear and started untying him. Talbot was soon at his side.

"Eli, I got your back whatever may come today, but we need to know what we're dealing with first. Might be nothing, but if it's something . . ." He paused, waiting for Elijah to look at him. "We are sorely outnumbered, and he ain't afraid to kill marshals, I don't think."

Elijah paused his frantic preparations and took a deep breath. When Talbot saw he had composed himself, he stood aside, and Elijah marched over to the other men. "Marshal, Talbot, I'll ask you two to hang at the edge of town and hope we get some kind of contact from Adams. Hobbs, see if you can't get you and your rifle on a roof across from the sheriff's office. I reckon they'll be along to see what is going on."

Elijah turned to Moses, wishing to convey in his eyes that there was nobody he trusted more in the world at a moment like this than his younger brother. "Mo, you and I will go see what's what with this fire."

The men all began to gather their things and check their saddles, and Marshal Foster soon saw both brothers pulling second revolvers out of their bags.

"You boys didn't leave much for the U.S. Army when you left their service, did you?"

Moses popped out the chamber and spun it, confirming the weapon was loaded before holstering it on his left hip. "Good thing, huh?" he said.

When the group was all mounted up, Marshal Foster spoke up. "We are operating as if Tucker has nothing to do with this until we know otherwise," he said. "I hate to use this analogy, all things considered, but so long as it remains peacetime, I'm in charge and I'd like to keep it that way. However"—he looked each man in the eye, stopping at Elijah—"should Frank Tucker decide he wants a war, Captain Barber will lead his troops."

"Off to the rooftop you go, Hobbs," Marshal Foster said in support of Elijah's plan.

Elijah and Moses were off next with yells to Bear and Copper. Elijah felt a strange calm come over him as the wind rushed into his face atop a running horse like in his days in the war. What had seemed like half an hour of talking and preparation had only been a matter of minutes. Looking over at his brother, he saw the look of determination he exhibited at no other time in life than when he was about to fight. They believed a righteous cause would win despite the odds and their situation.

Behind them, Marshal Foster and Talbot swung at a trot for the edge of town. "We're going to have a fight, aren't we?" Foster yelled loud enough for Talbot to hear him.

"We are, Marshal."

"God help us, Talbot."

"God and those Barber boys," Talbot answered.

Time to Dance

—•—

Elijah's worst fears were confirmed as he and Moses galloped into town and saw flames coming from Mary Adams's store. Elijah felt his cheeks become hot with rage as he skidded Bear to a stop out in front and slapped reins to a post.

"Mr. Barber! Mr. Barber!" Mary Adams came out of the building next door and ran to him, collapsing into his arms, coughing.

Elijah and Moses saw broken glass in each front window, the last bits of what looked like a torch lying on the floor below one of them.

"Did you see who done it, ma'am?" Moses was turning all around, looking for witnesses or a guilty party.

Still holding on to Mary, Elijah looked at Moses, hate in his eyes. "You know darn well who did it," he said.

Mary continued to cough, now shaking her head and waving her hands. She had been running around and had been in the building, Elijah thought. She began to speak, panting between words. "I tried to get word of George . . . was out telling people what was happening . . ." She summoned a giant breath. "John . . . John is in there."

Elijah threw Mary into Moses's arms and burst through the door into the growing smoke and flames. His eyes immediately stung, and he began to cough. He removed his coat, pulled a handkerchief from his pocket, tied it around his nose and mouth, and entered the inferno.

"John! Johnny!" Elijah began to feel his way around the store, attempting to remember how it had looked on previous visits. "It's Deputy Barber . . . Eli. Son, if you can hear me, I need you to call out so I can find you."

He stepped over a flaming shelf of goods that had fallen over in the center of the aisle, then tripped forward after catching his foot on a crate. He began crawling along hands and knees, coughing more violently now. His head bumped into what must have been the counter, and he sat himself up to lean against it.

"Johnny!" He called out, wheezing after he did. He began to worry he would be unable to hear the boy. The noise of the flames and cracking and falling wood was becoming too much. He could barely make out the square of pale light from the open doorway but thought he heard bits and pieces of Moses's voice yelling to him.

"Eli . . . get out . . . fire brigade."

Elijah summoned what felt like the last breath he could spare in his lungs and called out for the boy. He slid around the counter toward the back and heard the coughing.

"Eli." The boy's voice was just loud enough to be heard. Over and over, he called Elijah's name as his coughing continued.

The flames had increased to the point that Elijah at least now had light to see. Able to look into the doorway behind the counter, he saw two fallen beams burning and blocking it, and the boy curled up next to it, covering his face.

"John, I'm here," Elijah called. "Can you crawl under the beams? Will you fit?"

The boy said nothing but turned toward Elijah and shook his head slightly.

A board in the ceiling cracked loudly, embers showering down, and Elijah knew they had very little time. He looked into the shelves at the back of the counter and saw a stack of blankets. He began to gather them up and called out to the boy.

"John, I need you to listen close, 'cause we got to be getting out of here." He held the blankets before his chest, sitting on his knees. "I'm going to throw myself on top of those beams, and I want you to climb up and over me, then get low again. We'll get out together."

The boy was quiet, and Elijah mustered all his strength and patience. "Johnny, I need to know you hear me and that you're going to let me get you back to your mama waiting just outside."

"OK, Eli."

Elijah rolled forward to the doorway and threw his blanket-covered torso on top of the beams, which cracked some, dropping him closer to the ground with a grunt. "Now, Johnny!"

The boy pushed himself off the floor, and Elijah soon felt him crawling over the top of him and rolling off toward the counter. Elijah also rolled off and wrapped one of the blankets around the boy's backside, then on top of him. "Hold it closed best you can, and I'm gonna drag you out of here, Johnny."

The boy pulled the blankets close, and Elijah squatted down and began dragging the boy backward through the smoke and flames. Looking to his right, he saw a great deal of smoke and steam and realized the fire brigade had begun pouring water onto the wall facing the neighboring building. He craned his neck behind him and saw Moses moving toward him through the smoke and grabbing the other end of the blanket.

"Pick him up, Mo," Elijah coughed.

Moses snatched up the boy and made for the door as Elijah collapsed. A beam crashed down in the center of the store, and Moses turned back just before the doorway.

"Go!" Elijah shouted as he crawled on his belly toward the door. His lungs were burning, and he could no longer see. Then he felt rough hands grab his shirt and begin pulling and heard Moses's voice.

"Alright, brother, that's enough hero action." Moses got him clear of the building and poured a bucket of water from the horse trough on his head and sat him up.

Pulling in the fresh air, Elijah wiped his wet face with the handkerchief, then drank straight from the bucket. He was still coughing but felt his senses coming back to him. He saw Mary Adams crouching, crying, squeezing her boy like she would never let him go. She made eye contact with him and mouthed a *thank you*; Elijah briefly forgot about any suffering that had gone into the rescue effort.

Elijah saw his hat sitting on the boardwalk, planted it back on his head, then reached up his hand to Moses for help standing upright.

"You alright, Eli?" Moses was looking him over.

Elijah turned and looked back at the burning store. Though the fire had spread rapidly, the fire brigade had done enough to keep it from spreading to nearby buildings. It had run out of fuel and was dying out. The building would be a near-total loss.

"I'm fine," Elijah responded. He picked his coat up off the ground. He turned back to Moses and began dusting himself off. "I just need to get some fresh air in my—" He cut himself off as he looked across the street and saw the two men from in front of the sheriff's office the night before. While much of the town had awoken and been looking on in worry or concern, these two were performing more of an inspection of the situation. One of them caught Elijah looking and gave a wicked grin.

Elijah looked at Moses, who was returning his stare with angry eyes. "Are you with me, brother?"

"Yessir," Moses answered.

"We aren't starting it," Elijah said. He gestured to Mary Adams to move away from the thoroughfare. "If they wanna open the ball though, we'll dance. You see either of them move for a gun, you beat him to it."

The sun was over the horizon now, and what little was shining into the street was in the faces of Tucker's thugs, Elijah noticed. He looked up behind him, squinting at the roofs of the nearby buildings. He didn't see Hobbs but hoped he was there.

"Bad enough you'll take orders to burn a law-abiding citizen's business to the ground," Elijah shouted. "But to darn near kill a young boy in the process?" Elijah began walking across the street in his shirt sleeves with Moses a step behind and to his right.

The meaner-looking of the two men pushed himself off the post he was leaning on and spit tobacco. "Not sure what you mean, Deputy," he said. "Quite an accusation though. Glad you got him out."

"Guess I'm a better man than you, to have gone in," Elijah said.

Elijah and Moses stopped in the center of the street, the two thugs standing at the edge directly in front of them. A crowd was gathering, out of the line of any possible shooting, and Elijah also noticed faces in windows up and down the street.

"These two men right here," Elijah yelled, "burnt Mary Adams's store to the ground and near killed her boy to punish her for being kin of George Adams and to intimidate her into giving up her business." Elijah knew people had seen him pull the boy out of the fire, and obviously they could see the burning building. "In front of all these townsfolk, I say that if you tell me who ordered you to do it, no harm will come to you."

Elijah saw the mean-looking man's fingers twitch on his right hand and heard Moses take a deep breath. He remembered moments like this from the war. There was an almost otherworldly quiet, the only sound being your pounding heart over what you feared was about to happen. There was only the quiet now, though, and the *thing* hadn't happened yet.

"What's it going to be?" Elijah now realized his fingers were twitching. He saw the mean man's sidekick darting his eyes all over the place. The mean man stood perfectly still, however.

The mean man went for his gun, and Elijah heard Moses's revolver go off in his right ear, then heard the snap of a wild round over his head. His eyes shifted to the right, the mean man falling to the ground in his peripheral vision as he watched the sidekick draw his weapon.

"Drop it!" Elijah yelled as he closed the distance between them, pointing the gun at the man's head. "Drop it or join your friend!" The man dropped to his knees, the gun falling before him. Elijah stuck it in his back and put a boot on the man's neck.

Elijah moved the gun to his left hand and pulled the one on his left hip with his right. He heard movement from around the corner of the building and shot a man that emerged with a rifle raised while keeping his other gun on his prisoner. Elijah had begun to scan the street when a door swung open, and a shotgun barrel emerged, leveling at Moses. "Mo, on your right!"

Elijah heard the crack of a rifle, and then the shotgun clattered to the ground, a man falling on top of it. It was Hobbs on the roof across the street.

Moses backed himself to where Elijah stood with his boot on the man's neck, scanning the street. "What now, Eli?"

Elijah holstered one revolver, then snatched the man by the collar and dragged him across the street to where Bear and Copper were. "Get that rope from the camp out of your bag, Mo."

Moses backed his way toward Elijah and the horses while scanning up and down the street with his revolvers.

Elijah looked up and found Hobbs on the roof while Moses got the rope out. "Better find a new perch," he called up. "Center of town." He saw Hobbs nod and disappear, then heard the sound of hoof beats behind him and swung around with a revolver raised.

"What on earth is going on?" Marshal Foster climbed down from his horse and scanned the street and its three bodies, a look of horror on his face when he saw the man under Elijah's boot and Moses bringing out a rope.

"You two got somewhere safe and out of the way you can get to?" Elijah was looking at Mary and Johnny, poking their heads around the corner of a neighboring building. She didn't respond; she simply gathered up her boy and began moving down an alley with him.

"What are you gonna do, Eli?" Talbot's voice was the quietest Elijah had ever heard. The gravelly sound almost drowned out the words.

"Elijah, I told you we didn't want to go starting a war if we could keep the peace," Marshal Foster scolded.

"Marshal," Elijah said, "Tucker started this war when he killed that bank assistant and those Pinkertons." He turned and looked at the smoldering building. "Or when they burned this innocent woman's store to the ground." He used a revolver to point at the dead men across the street. "Or when they pulled on Mo and me for asking them what they done."

Elijah looked at Talbot, then stared at Marshal Foster with wide eyes. Getting no response, he holstered his revolver, then stood his prisoner in front of Moses, who was holding the rope. "Hands in front," Elijah commanded him. The man raised his hands without hesitation; he was trembling. "Tie 'em up real tight and give me a lead," Elijah said. Then he turned to Marshal Foster and Talbot. "I'm giving Tucker one last chance to admit who he is in front of all these people."

All Over Again

"I think you're out on your own hook here, Eli." Moses was trailing behind Elijah, leading Copper and Bear. "I'm with you, brother, but I need to know what your plan is."

Up ahead, Elijah was pulling his prisoner along and taking note of all the townspeople watching their procession. The fact that he was now the one immersed in this life after not wanting to leave home was not lost on him. He began to see Tucker's guns emerge along the street and boardwalks, thankful they were too afraid of their boss to start shooting of their own accord.

"I'm calling Tucker out in front of the town, and this fella is gonna tell everyone what he done and who ordered it." He turned and stared at the timid prisoner and gave his rope a jerk.

Elijah stopped for a moment and caught eyes with Marshal Foster and Talbot. He glanced up at the roof of the sheriff's office across the street, a couple of buildings from the saloon. The two followed his eyes and saw Matt Hobbs crouched down, holding his rifle.

"I'll hold the horses here," the marshal said. "Isn't that how it works in the cavalry?"

"Sounds like a fine idea, Marshal," Talbot said. He grabbed the reins from Moses, then handed his own over to Marshal Foster.

Elijah began walking again, wondering why Talbot covered for the marshal, who wanted no part of being in a dangerous situation.

Moses hurried after his brother. "Eli, we are outgunned here by more'n a few, even with those fellas back there out of action. What if they start shootin'?"

"Then it'll be pretty obvious what kind of outfit they are," Elijah replied to his brother without turning around or stopping. His eyes were locked straight ahead, focused on reaching the front of the Blue Union.

"Lot of good that will do us, dead in the street," Moses replied.

"Then let's not allow that to happen, Moses."

Elijah stopped in front of the saloon and centered his prisoner before it. Looking down the street, he saw at least a half dozen of Tucker's guns and briefly doubted his actions. He didn't have any tactical high ground, so he would have to hope a moral one ruled the day. He shook off the thought; this was how it would happen now.

"Frank Tucker!" Elijah's voice bellowed in a commanding tone he had not summoned since the war. "Show yourself." There was some stirring in the front of the saloon and murmurs of voices nearby.

"Lot of horses tied up out front for this early in the morning," Moses remarked.

Elijah now noticed it, too—all of them with empty rifle scabbards.

There was more shuffling near the front of the Blue Union, and then a door opened and out walked three men: Frank Tucker, Charlie Wade, and a man Elijah didn't recognize, with a rifle at his side. Tucker didn't have his usual hat or jacket, just a tie and braces. He was wiping his face with a towel.

"You'll forgive me, Deputy. I was in the middle of a shave. I hate to appear in front of the fine people of Rockville unkempt." He finished wiping off his face, then made a production of leaning forward and squinting. "If you'd like one as well, my barber is the best."

Elijah resisted the urge to rub his face and jerked the rope to bring his prisoner up alongside him.

"Ah, have you caught another one of Parke County's vigilantes? Well done." Tucker clapped his hands. "Please give our U.S. Marshals a round of applause, everyone." There was a smattering of weak applause by some of Tucker's men and a few confused onlookers. The rifleman and Charlie Wade stared straight ahead.

"One of the men you had burn Mary Adams's grocery to the ground," Elijah responded.

"One of?"

Elijah sensed the slightest bit of trepidation from Tucker. He never failed to put on a show for the townspeople, but you could catch his concern if you were looking for it.

Moses jerked his head toward where the shooting had occurred. "The other one's back there in the street where he threw down on me," Moses said. "Mustered out permanently, I reckon."

Tucker looked Moses over, then Elijah saw him glance down the street before exchanging a quick look with Charlie Wade.

"Two others thought it'd be clever to pull on us and met the same fate." Elijah noticed some of the townspeople whispering to each other. "A sight witnessed by many a resident of Rockville."

"Heavy accusations, Deputy," Tucker said. "Furthermore, if there are men of this town pulling weapons on U.S. Marshals, I suggest we get the sheriff involved." He stood up tall and craned his neck toward the sheriff's office. "Alas, he has abandoned his post after releasing a dangerous prisoner. Haven't seen him, though. Have you, Barber?" Tucker's smirk made Elijah's blood boil.

Someone brought Tucker his coat and hat, and he thanked them and put them on. “You know, Deputy Barber, before the U.S. Marshals showed up in town, we didn’t have these issues. Rockville has been growing and prospering since the war ended, but since your arrival, we’ve had violence in the streets, a sheriff abandon his post, and now a terrible fire that appears was no accident.”

“You know an awful lot about that fire for just having finished a shave,” Elijah said.

Tucker just glared at Elijah’s prisoner.

Elijah glanced around to understand how onlookers reacted to Tucker’s speech. At best, he continued to get the feeling that people were too afraid to do anything about the reality of Frank Tucker.

“Now, I’m not the law, Deputy Barber, but as a respected leader of the town, I may have to do something. We’ve got renegade U.S. Marshals and an abandoned sheriff’s post. This a dire situation that may require something to be done, for we have worked too hard to lose what is ours.”

“You mean you’ve done too much evil to lose what you’ve stolen,” Talbot said.

Tucker looked at Talbot and spoke just loud enough for those nearby to hear. “Prove it, old man.”

Elijah narrowed his eyes at Tucker and his re-emerging devilish grin. He stuck his foot into the back of his prisoner’s knee, and the man fell.

“Who told you to burn the store down? Nearly kill the boy? Shoot at us if we showed up?”

The man began to shake and mutter but did not speak.

“This is hardly the decorum for—”

“Who ordered you to do it?” Elijah’s said loudly, cutting Tucker off. He yanked on the rope, causing the man to fall forward.

The man returned to his knees and began to mutter, and Elijah stuck his ear nearer him. "Speak up so they can all hear you." He pulled his revolver out and saw all of Tucker's men lift their weapons as well.

Elijah saw Moses slowly remove each of his revolvers, and Talbot pulled his.

"I don't want any shooting," Elijah said in a commanding voice. He looked at the prisoner. "I just want you to tell all of us who ordered you to do what you did."

The man struggled to his feet, pushing off the ground with his bound hands. He looked Elijah in the eyes, and it appeared to Elijah that he had resigned himself to doing the right thing. The man turned back to the saloon and opened his mouth to speak.

Elijah heard the shot ring out and saw his prisoner slump. Turning to the saloon, he saw that the rifleman next to Tucker had been the one to fire. The rifleman had begun to scan the street, seeking to defend himself when another shot rang out and the rifleman fell. The shot had come from Hobbs on a roof across from the saloon. Citizens yelled and screamed as they fled the street.

Elijah dropped the rope he no longer needed for his dead prisoner and pulled his second revolver, firing at a man aiming at him from the front steps of the saloon. Out of the corner of his eye he saw Moses firing toward but missing Wade who was covering Tucker's retreat into the saloon.

The two brothers backed up to each other, both of them with their revolvers raised. Two men emerged from the saloon with guns high, and Elijah dropped them both with a shot from each pistol. He peered through the saloon's doorway and saw Tucker pointing and saying something before heading up some stairs. Then he saw the nine armed men whose mounts were out front marching toward the entrance.

"He brought in some backup," Elijah said to Moses. He heard one of Moses's revolvers fire. "We gotta fall back to the sheriff's office."

"Got it," Moses yelled.

The two brothers began hurriedly backing away from the saloon. Elijah looked to his left. "Talbot, we're falling back to the—" He was interrupted by Talbot firing his weapon, then a second shot from near the saloon, followed by Talbot's shoulder jerking backward.

Elijah heard Hobbs's rifle crack and assumed the shot was intended for Talbot's attacker. He hurried across the street to Talbot, who was holding a hand near his armpit and mumbling to himself. There was already a lot of blood, but he was on his feet.

"I'm fine; let's go," Talbot managed.

The trio resumed their movement toward the sheriff's office, occasionally sending a shot back toward the saloon. Tucker's men did not pursue, however; they all looked up toward Hobbs and found cover.

Elijah, Moses, and Talbot burst into the sheriff's office to find Marshal Foster and the young deputy.

"Clear off that table," Elijah commanded. The deputy knocked things to the floor, and Talbot stopped him.

"You got a sawbones in here gonna patch me up?" Talbot was grimacing and lifting his arm to look at his injury. "Not much you can do about that spot."

"You gonna be alright, Talbot?" Moses was looking out the window but turned back to face him.

"I'll be fine, Mo," he said. He sat down on the edge of the desk with a grunt and looked at Marshal Foster. "I'm fine."

The marshal nodded in a way Elijah thought was trying to convince himself and joined Moses at the window. Elijah stared straight ahead at Talbot.

The old sheriff was looking down at the bright red blood soaking through the whole left side of his shirt. He looked up at Elijah and pursed his lips. Then Talbot shook his head in a way that seemed to indicate to Elijah that he was already dead.

"We can wait all day," a taunting voice came from the outside.

Elijah stared ahead blankly at Talbot. *This is Pilot Knob all over again*, he thought.

Final Goodbye

Elijah paced the sheriff's office while the armed men down the street occasionally hollered in their direction or took a shot at the front of the building. The young deputy, whose name they learned was Thomas Owens, was helping Moses remove some boards from the ceiling to allow them to communicate better with Hobbs. Or, as they had all noted, to possibly escape from.

The group had found some old shirts and cloth and tied them around Talbot's shoulder and under his arm. The bleeding had slowed, but the wound was in an awkward spot that any movement made worse.

They had minimal water and some stowed-away food that was maybe enough for one man to last a day or two. Elijah knew the longer they stayed holed up in the office, the worse their situation would get.

He stopped his pacing at a desk where Marshal Foster was writing intently. "What you working on, Marshal?"

Marshal Foster took a deep breath, then looked up with resignation. "Not that they won't just take everything, but it's a statement of everything that has happened and a letter to my wife."

Elijah bit his lip and looked away for a moment. He knew it was a bit of a futile effort as well and was upset at the marshal's outward admission of doom, but he supposed he couldn't blame him.

"Eli." Talbot's voice came softly from the opposite corner. They had pushed a desk against the wall so he could sit up with his back supported. Elijah looked at him, and Talbot gestured toward an empty chair beside the desk.

Elijah put a hand on the marshal's shoulder. "I'll leave you to it." The marshal's hesitations over the last days, his seeming desire to avoid conflict, and the revelation he had misled them about his war service had soured Elijah on the man. Looking at him now, however, he remembered the man's honest service attempts and realized he might have avoided this mess if he'd been left to his own devices.

Elijah pulled the chair over just before Talbot and sat, looking up into the man's eyes. They had a look of sadness he had never seen from him.

Talbot glanced at Moses and the deputy, who were passing some ammunition and rifles to Hobbs, then Marshal Foster, who was focused on his writing. He looked down at Elijah. "They're either lying to themselves or ignorant, but surely you realize I'm not going to make it?"

Elijah opened his eyes wide.

"It ain't yet stopped bleeding, only slowed down some. Caught a dang stray in the underarm and that's gonna be what does me in." He wrinkled his nose and squinted his eyes, and Elijah wondered if the old sheriff wasn't fighting back tears.

"Maybe if we can get you somewhere? Or get someone here?"

Talbot just shook his head. "Don't think it's gonna matter, son."

Elijah thought the way he said son was different than any time he had before. An emphasis and sincerity seemed to convey a different meaning than in the past. Elijah wiped a tear from his eye with his thumb and looked away as he tried to hide it.

"You're going to listen to me now," Talbot said. "You didn't get any last words from your pa, and I wasn't there to give any to my son." He sat up as tall as he could, grimacing.

Elijah took off his hat, ran a hand through his hair, then leaned forward and nodded, clearing his throat to keep from crying.

"You need to realize that, especially for people of little means like us, we need all the help we can get. I know you think men like your father or me are strong and independent and don't want anyone in our business. If your folks hadn't supported me when my wife died though . . ." He trailed off and cleared his throat. "Dammit, boy."

Elijah had never heard the man swear before, and it made him chuckle through the tears.

Talbot composed himself and continued. "Or if I hadn't taken care of you and Mo and your ma when your daddy died . . ." He trailed off again, the point being made. "I don't know if you feel like you owe all that to others then, but you done all you could for that farm and in that war. Anyone who thinks some farm boy going off to serve without any experience wasn't going to make mistakes is a fool."

Elijah saw Moses look over at them with concern, and he waved him over.

"What I'm saying, Eli, is to take the help where you can get it. You're a natural leader, and a smart man what for hardly having any formal learning. You can read and write and served your country in a war. Well done, Elijah Barber; you've bested everyone in your family who come before you."

Elijah smiled.

Moses joined them, and Talbot gave him a nod. "You don't have to do it all, though, is what I'm saying. Now I wish I knew how you were gonna get out of this, but knowing you two, you'll find a way. Lean on each other though, and whoever else decides to help as well."

The brothers looked at each other. Moses was now fighting back tears as well.

Talbot looked at Elijah. "You done far better helping him become a man than you give yourself credit for." He turned to Moses. "Or that you give him credit for, Mo."

Both brothers smiled.

"Find yourselves a way out of this together," Talbot said. "Don't you dare let worrying about me slow it down though. You stop Tucker, give these people their lives back, and bury me right here so they have a reminder what we done for 'em."

Elijah stood and took the hand of Talbot's good arm. "Thank you." He wiped away more tears. "For everything."

Talbot waved his hand as if the emotions were a fly he could shoo away. "Ain't nothing easy in this life, Eli. Bad people do bad things, dang it; good people do bad things, too." He spoke in a low voice. "You and your brother, you got it in you to do the things nobody else will do to make things right, though."

Talbot squeezed Elijah's hand, and the two men looked at each other, at peace with the finality of things.

"Got someone coming up the street toward us," Marshal Foster said. He leaned forward at the desk, looking out the window.

Elijah and Moses drew their revolvers, and Talbot gingerly reached for his.

Marshal Foster looked back at all of them. "Not from the saloon, from the other direction." The marshal stood and looked more closely. "It's a woman in a dress."

Moses hurried over, careful not to stand directly in front of the glass, and peered down the street. "Well, I'll be," he said. "That's Clara White."

Lady in the Dress

Clara White walked along the sheriff's building side of the street carrying a large reticule bag. Elijah heard voices from the other end of the main street calling out as she got closer.

"Ma'am it's best you not be here," came the loudest one.

"I must urgently speak to the sheriff," Clara called out. "I've heard so much shooting, and I cannot find my son."

Elijah watched her get closer to them and thought that at this distance and in a dress, none of the men would recognize her if they had seen her before.

"Sheriff Miller skedaddled, ma'am."

"You best stay away," said another voice. "Those renegade marshals are holed up there, and we aim to take the town back."

"Oh, dear," Clara said. She glanced toward the building, making eye contact with all of them through the window. "So, the shooting started, and he just ran out the side of the building, got on his horse, and rode off?"

"She's trying to tell us something," Moses said.

Elijah turned from the window and looked at Marshal Foster. "Where did you tie up the horses?"

The marshal seemed startled by the urgency of Elijah's question. "When the shooting started, I brought them around to the side of the building."

Elijah and Moses looked at each other with raised eyebrows.

"Thomas, you got a side door to the alley?" Elijah was back to the window listening for Clara's instructions.

"Yessir, in the middle hallway between the office and the cells."

"Why would she think anyone could just sneak out and ride off?" Marshal Foster was rubbing his chin and looking back and forth between the Barber brothers.

"Shh, quiet." Elijah had missed some of the back and forth with Clara and Tucker's men but wanted to ensure he followed it correctly.

"Well, that doesn't make much sense to me," Clara said. "I suppose he had a good reason to do that when the shooting began, though." She looked at the window again. "Did he take his deputy with? I hope he took his deputy with."

"That's it," Moses said. "She wants two of us to come out when the shooting starts."

Elijah nodded and walked to the hole in the roof. "You hearing this, Hobbs?"

"I can't say I follow," the Pinkerton replied. "I'm ready for whatever happens, though."

When Marshal Foster caught Elijah's eye, Elijah and Moses were reloading their weapons. "You sure about this?" Foster said.

Elijah holstered his revolvers and took a deep breath. "If it's a trap, I reckon it hurries up what was already going to happen."

Marshal Foster scratched his chin and seemed to consider this. "I suppose that's right. I'll stay with Talbot, and we'll await what happens."

Talbot stood with great effort and pulled his revolver. He shuffled toward the door, then turned to see the group looking at him.

"If you all think I'm gonna die sitting in the corner after taking a stray bullet, then you don't know me none."

"Ma'am," a voice called from the street. "I'm going to have to ask you to head on back home."

"Alright then," she said. "Can I leave something for if the sheriff returns, though?" She looked toward the window for a long moment, then opened the strings on the bag. Falling to the ground, her hands appeared with a revolver in each, and she began firing down the street.

Elijah and Moses hurried to the side door and into the alley, finding Bear and Copper tied up. Loosing their reins, the brothers swung into their saddles and kicked the horses toward the street.

Tucker's men were caught off guard and delayed in shooting back as Clara began creating distance, moving between cover positions along the boardwalk. There was more gunfire when Elijah and Moses barreled into the street, and Tucker's men began mounting their horses.

Clara was behind a post emptying her revolvers when she saw the brothers coming. She stepped into the street and smiled at Moses, who reached a hand down as he passed and swung her up behind him. Clara pulled Moses's revolver from his holster and, wrapping one arm around him, turned and began firing at their pursuers.

"Toward the tree line just outside town," she yelled. She fired three quick shots; one of the pursuing riders fell from his saddle.

Elijah turned to see Matt Hobbs firing rapidly from the roof, dropping one of Tucker's men. Just before turning back, he saw the door to the sheriff's office swing open and a staggering Talbot Jones firing into the group as it passed.

Clearing the last buildings of the town, the ground in front of them opened up wide into a grassy area. Elijah looked at Moses and saw Clara replacing his shot-out revolver. He saw the tree line up ahead and wondered what was supposed to be happening. "What's the plan, Clara?" He was growing anxious that this was a trap.

"Keep going," she yelled.

The brothers each gave a yell, and Bear and Copper responded with even more speed. The ground rose slightly just in front of them, and when they were on the downward slope, Elijah saw the slightest opening in the tree line. Looking into it, he saw a man desperately waving his hat, signaling to come that way.

"There he is—that's George," Clara shouted. "Ride straight through him."

The occasional bullet still zipped by the three of them. Reaching the tree line, they slowed their horses to navigate the trees, and Elijah heard George Adams shouting orders.

"Up! Up men!"

They got Bear and Copper stopped and turned around, and Clara jumped off, pulling the dress over her head and revealing the men's clothes they had seen her in before. Without a word, she rushed toward her horse.

Moving back to the edge of the tree line, Elijah saw most of the original group of Adams's men and a handful more.

"Get ready," Adams yelled to his men.

Tucker's men came into view at the edge of the tree line, their horses skidding to a stop at the realization of what had happened.

"Fire!"

George Adams's small army unleashed a volley of fire, creating the near-simultaneous pop of rifles Elijah had not heard since the war.

"Huzzah!" Moses yelled. He was waving his hat in the air, watching many of them fall and others frantically trying to turn around in the trees. He looked toward Elijah.

Elijah said nothing, only yelling and kicking Bear, who began picking his way through the trees. He saw George Adams give him a grin, then start moving toward his horse tied up nearby.

Emerging into the open ground, Elijah encouraged Bear and tightened his slouch hat on his head. The smell of gunpowder in the air while he galloped across the open land on a horse put Elijah in a familiar state of mind and gave him a confidence he often lacked. Slowing his horse, he pulled the Spencer from its scabbard, working the lever with one hand and scanning for targets.

Turning to his right, he saw a man raise a revolver toward him, and he quickly aimed and fired, dropping the man from his saddle. A rider nearby looked up in surprise, and before he could aim his weapon, Elijah levered in another round and fired again to the same effect. Turning to his left, he saw Moses having similar success, most of Tucker's group panicking in confusion.

Elijah turned Bear around and saw one of Adams's men off his horse, in a brawl with one of Tucker's men who had been knocked from his. The two tumbled in the grass until Tucker's man got the upper hand. Elijah began to ride in their direction and saw the thug reach a knife into the air to plunge into his adversary when Clara White rode up and dispatched him.

She gave Elijah a nod, then pointed toward town. Turning in that direction, he saw the remaining two riders hightailing it back to Rockville. Elijah, Moses, and Adams's group converged.

"Just like Gettysburg?" Elijah allowed himself a smile recollecting their earlier conversation.

"More or less," George Adams replied.

Elijah looked back and realized one of Adams's men had been killed, and he removed his hat. "No matter what, we come back for him. He sacrificed for our—for your—cause."

Adams squinted toward the fallen man. "Bill was a good fella," he said. "I'll be sure to talk to his wife."

Elijah looked around at the group. In addition to Clara and himself, Adams had seven men. "We were worried you hightailed it after being sprung from the jail, but looks like you were recruiting?"

"Yes, indeed," Adams said. "Though it turns out it was one of our originals ratted us out to Tucker and took a payment to tell him where I was."

Elijah shook his head. "That explains how he's handled all this and how he got the extra men here so fast." Elijah hesitated, then asked, "What's become of that man, then?"

"No longer an issue," Adams answered quickly.

Elijah ran a hand through his hair, then put his slouch hat back on his head. He'd overlook the extrajudicial action in light of the situation.

"Sheriff ain't come back?" Adams asked.

"Not yet at least," Elijah answered.

"I don't think we should wait to chase them in," Moses said. He was already reloading his weapon, and others began doing the same. "That wasn't all of them."

"We'll show some force," Elijah said. "We ride hard back into town, two by two." He quickly counted their number to eleven. "We'll form into two lines of five; let 'em know we plan to finish the job if they won't surrender. George, I don't mean to put you front and center for any shooting, but this is your town, and I offer you the spot at the front of the lines."

George sat up straight in his saddle. "It's my honor."

"And if they want to fight?" asked Clara.

"Moses and I will charge ahead and give them hell with our repeaters," Elijah said. "You all dismount and start finding targets and moving toward the saloon. We'll circle back and join you."

"Use the buildings and any cover we can find to move down the street toward the saloon," George said. "I don't know where they'll come from, but we can use crossfire to our advantage. I think we've close to evened up their man advantage, so we don't need to get clever. We'll be smart."

"One last thing," Elijah said. "The marshals are still here on law business, and this ain't no war, even if it feels like it." He made eye contact with everyone in the group. "If someone isn't shooting or offers themselves up, we take them in. Marshal Foster and the deputy sheriff are in the office and can guard them."

There were nods and murmurs of understanding.

Elijah wanted to ensure this point was driven home. "I ain't exactly sure on the legality of this, but everyone that isn't Moses raise your right hand."

The group exchanged glances and then raised their hands.

"Do you promise to act as a deputized U.S. Marshal, uphold the law, and follow orders?"

They all nodded.

"Let's hope that doesn't come up," Elijah said. He saw George Adams laugh and Clara smile.

After a moment of quiet, Moses spoke up. "Anyone have a bugle?"

There were chuckles in the group. For once, Elijah was glad his brother could bring humor to a heavy moment.

Elijah turned Bear back toward town, and the group lined up behind him. Turning his head, he shouted, "Let's go get your town back."

The Lieutenant

The rounds started coming their way as they approached the town, and Elijah and Moses got small in their saddles, hoping those behind them would follow suit. One snapped by Elijah's ear, and he looked over at Moses. "Those are close," he shouted.

"They've got a Sharps rifles I reckon," Moses hollered. "He won't miss again."

The words had barely cleared Moses's lips when they heard the pained, high-pitched whinny of George Adams's horse and saw the animal crash to the ground, Adams tumbling forward in a heap. Elijah and Moses went racing by, and Elijah looked Adams over the best he could.

"Just the horse," Elijah shouted to Moses. He started angling off to the right and looked behind him to see the courageous group was keeping up. He got even lower in the saddle and patted Bear on the neck. "I can let you out of here soon, boy," he said.

Elijah looked left to see Moses moving away from him to the other side of the thoroughfare and saw he was hanging off the left side of his saddle. Feeling another round whip past his head, Elijah copied the maneuver. "Come on, Bear; almost there."

Reaching the end of town, Elijah reined Bear to as fast a stop as his speed allowed and quickly swung out of his saddle. Pulling the

Spencer from its scabbard, he jerked the horse's reins to face back toward the tree line and slapped him on the rump. "Go on, Bear. Go on!" Seeming to sense it was for his own good, the horse trotted off.

"Gotta find this shooter before we move ahead anymore," Elijah shouted to Moses.

Elijah leaned his back against a beam in front of a store and levered a round into the Spencer. The rider behind him arrived where Elijah had dismounted and got down from his horse. However, he began looking for somewhere to tie it up, and Elijah gestured for him to let it go. "You gotta get—"

Elijah heard the shot an instant before the man dropped to the ground. He hung his head. Then he heard another shot almost immediately, and another posse member went down.

"Dang it, Eli, there's two of 'em," Moses yelled. He dared a peek into the street and then hollered up to Hobbs. "Got anything up there?"

Hobbs stuck his head up and a round splintered wood near the top of the sheriff's office.

"Out front of the blacksmith shop!" Moses yelled. The shop was on his side of the street. There was an area out front full of crates, and a supply wagon was parked there. "Holed up behind them crates or that wagon."

"Everyone back behind the buildings." Elijah waved them all away. "Hobbs, get ready. Mo, cover me." Elijah took a deep breath and then ran into the street toward Moses. A round threw up dirt before him, then he heard the crack of Hobbs's rifle from the roof.

He arrived up against the building, breathing hard. Moses just glared at him. "Didn't really give me a chance to cover you."

"Got one!" Hobbs yelled. "Still don't see the other."

Elijah peered into the window of the building they were leaning against. "I hope there's a back exit," he said. "We'll go out around back, move through the alley, and clean out the blacksmith shop."

Moses shook his head incredulously. "This would have been a really poor plan if you were laying in the street right now."

"Like them?" Elijah responded. He looked at the two bodies. Then he saw George Adams limping up to join the group gathering behind the buildings at the end of the street. Elijah did his best with gestures to show what they were doing, and Adams nodded. He couldn't believe the man was still fighting after all he had been through. *He wants his life back.*

They left the carbines in front of the building, entered the store, and found a back door. Elijah and Moses leaned against opposite sides of the frame and looked at each other.

"Who goes fir—?"

"I will," Elijah interjected.

"Trying to get killed today?" Moses asked. He removed his hat, wiped his brow, and stuck it back on. "Fine." He stared at Elijah. "If I was them, I'd have at least a couple'a men guarding the back entrance to this holed-up shooter. You get clear of the door quick and look left, and I'll look right."

Elijah nodded at him, a bit of pride in his eyes. "Alright, here we go."

Elijah kicked open the door, getting out of Moses's way, and turned to his left, pistols raised. He saw nobody there and spun back to the right when he heard a shot.

"He ducked back into the blacksmith!" Moses yelled.

The brothers moved slowly toward the back of the blacksmith shop, guns raised, scanning windows, alleys, and doorways for any of Tucker's men. They looked at each other for the second time in a few minutes while holding up opposite sides of a door frame. They heard another shot from the Sharps rifle out front, and Elijah cringed.

"My turn," Moses said. He pushed open the door and entered. Elijah entered in behind him, his eyes trying to adjust to the dark back of the shop.

"I saw him duck in—"

Moses's voice was cut off by a loud crash, a growling noise from another man, and then a grunt from Moses. Elijah strained to find the scuffle in the low light. He located the two men wrestling, Moses trying to pry the other man's gun out of his hand. Out of the corner of his eye, he thought he saw someone ducking behind a bench full of tools. He tried to keep an eye out for the lurking man while also watching Moses.

Moses got the gun out of his attacker's hand, but the man pinned him down. He pressed an arm into Moses's neck, brought a fist down on his face, then gave him a blow to the body before pressing his arm in harder.

"Drop the gun or I'll kill him," the attacker said. Keeping his arm on Moses's neck, he pulled a knife from his waist.

"Let him up, or I shoot," Elijah said. The two of them were nearly one, and at a fair distance in low light, Elijah was unsure of his threat.

The lurking man popped up on the other side of the shop, his gun trained on Elijah. "Better do what he says."

"Eli . . . just go . . ."

Elijah could hear Moses struggling for breath between his pained words, but squinting in the low light, he could also see him stretching out his fingers toward his attacker's dropped revolver. "OK," Elijah said. "OK." He stalled for an additional second, and when he saw Moses's hand grasp the gun, Elijah fired a shot into the attacker's head. He dropped to the floor and rolled aside as the lurking man fired a wild round past him. Just as the man was scanning to find him, Elijah heard the click of a hammer, a deep lung-filling breath of air from Moses, and the sound of a revolver firing.

Elijah looked up from the ground and saw Moses's attacker lying dead and Moses struggling to his feet. The lurking man was lying on his side, grasping at the wound in the top of his chest, just below the neck, where Moses had shot him. Moses walked past the man to the crate he had emerged from behind. Reaching down behind it, he produced the Sharps rifle.

Elijah walked over and stood directly over the man. "How many people did you kill today because your boss wouldn't let them live free in their own town?" Elijah asked.

The man could barely speak, gurgling noises coming from his throat. "Help me," he managed. His eyes were wide, staring at Elijah.

"I couldn't even if I wanted to," Elijah said. Then he raised his revolver and ended it.

Moses had been watching but looked away when Elijah pulled the trigger. He murmured softly and looked back.

"Had to be done," Elijah said.

"Don't make it easier," Moses replied.

"I know." Elijah looked him over. "You OK?"

Moses nodded. "Thank you for—"

Elijah held a hand up. "You did the same."

Moses nodded, then dusted himself off. "Maybe I shouldn't have gone to breakfast after all the other day."

The brothers looked at each other for a moment, shared a smile, then remembered their work wasn't done, no matter the experience they'd just had. They crept to the front of the blacksmith shop, now in the light of the outside, and scanned the area where the shooters had been.

"Coming out," Elijah yelled. "George, let's move everyone up on the boardwalks. Keep covered best you can."

Moses kicked the boot of the shooter Hobbs had dropped. He looked up to where the Pinkerton had been firing from. "Nice shootin' for a fancy East Coast fella."

They both looked up, guns raised, when they heard a door open. Then they saw the sheriff's door open slowly from across the street to see that Hobbs had come down from the roof to join the fight on the street. Then, surprisingly, he saw Sheriff Miller walk out behind them.

"Let's finish this," Hobbs said.

The remaining vigilante group members had lined up in the street, ready to march. Most of them were looking at Sheriff Miller. "Thank you for coming back," Clara White said. George Adams nodded his agreement.

"Thank Mary," the sheriff replied. "She came to the house and gave me a real talking to."

Elijah looked at Hobbs and raised an eyebrow. "Talbot?"

Matt Hobbs just shook his head.

Elijah took a deep breath, and Moses lowered his head.

"We'll surround the saloon," Elijah called out. "If he's still here, he'll have nowhere to go." He looked back to the dead shooter lying next to his rifle. "I reckon these fellas were given the task of slowing us done while he skedaddled, so let's not waste any time."

A shot splintered a wooden sign above the brothers' heads, and they instinctively crouched. The entire posse was returning fire as what Elijah assumed had to be the last of Tucker's remaining crew moved down the street, shooting as they went.

Elijah turned to his brother and put a hand on his shoulder. "Mo, lead these people to take their town back."

Moses stared at him wide-eyed. "What are you going to—"

Elijah cut him off. "I'm still going for him." He checked the loads in his revolvers, stuffing them back into their holsters and looking up at the distance to the saloon. "Let's make sure this ends now. Go lead. You're my lieutenant. You should have been a long time ago."

Moses pulled Elijah's head toward his so their foreheads were touching, their hats falling off. "What a life we've had, brother," Moses said.

"What a life," Elijah echoed. "Let's make this a new beginning and not the end, though."

Elijah saw one of Adams's men stand to move to a different position and take a bullet to the chest. He pushed his brother toward the group's makeshift firing line, and Moses took off in a low crouch, grabbing their rifles from George Adams as he passed. "We'll cover you," he called back.

Elijah pulled his slouch hat back on and backed against a building. He watched Moses fearlessly walk up and down the posse's firing line giving orders, stepping into the lieutenant role that should have been his back in the war. Elijah allowed himself a moment of pride.

Finally, Moses looked back at him. "Ready?"

Elijah pulled both revolvers, glanced toward the saloon, then back at his brother.

He took a deep breath. "Ready."

Blue Union

Moses and the group opened up with everything they had, and Elijah began moving down the boardwalk toward the saloon. One of Tucker's men turned to him from the street at the same time one appeared in front of him, and he sent a shot from each revolver in both directions, one of their shots splintering the wood of a building behind him.

Gunshots, yells, and the hollering of commands raged behind him, but Elijah made it to the saloon's door. Peeking in a window, he did not see or hear anything. He made a mental note that he had five rounds in each gun. Taking a deep breath, he kicked the door in.

His eyes took a second to adjust to the lower light of the saloon, but a scan of the large barroom didn't reveal anyone. "Frank Tucker," he called out, "your time is up."

A man popped up from behind the bar with a shotgun, and Elijah dove behind a table and chairs, the door behind where he'd previously stood splintering. The man fired a second shot toward the table but didn't have the right angle. Elijah heard the man crack open the shotgun to reload and rose and ran for the bar, firing into his chest as he snapped it shut again.

Elijah dropped to the ground and sat against the end of the bar. "You're running out of thugs, Frank." He heard the shooting dying down outside and becoming more sporadic. "Based on how I left things, my money is on my brother's side for how that gunfight in the street is wrapping up."

Elijah heard booted feet trying to creep on the wood-planked floor and peeked out into the room. A shot zipped past his face, and he reached above the counter and fired off two shots with the revolver in his right hand. He quickly moved in a crouch behind the length of the bar, hoping the man was focusing on where he had just fired from.

Emerging at the other side, he stuck his head out and saw the man moving to where he had previously been. He popped up and shot at the man with the pistol in his left hand. He missed, and the man spun around and fired a wild shot, bottles shattering. Elijah ducked behind the bar for cover, then re-emerged from a different position, firing a shot from each gun but missing again as the man dove behind a table. He cursed himself for being so wild with his shots. *Down to two in each,* he thought.

The man had gone quiet, apparently tired of giving his position away with his steps. Elijah took a deep breath, then looked down and saw a large portion of one of the broken bottles. Picking it up by the neck, he tossed it to the other side of the bar. When the man stood and leaned over the bar to fire, Elijah emerged and shot him in the side. The man fell to the ground, and Elijah was forced to use another round when he reached for his gun.

He flipped open the revolver chamber in his left hand and removed the final cartridge, transferring it to the right, then holstering. *Enough wasting rounds with your off hand, Eli.*

"We got things under control down there?" It was Tucker's voice calling from a room upstairs.

Elijah considered saying "All good, boss" in Wade's voice but had no idea if he was here. Instead, he crept as quietly as he could to the stairs and began making his way up while hugging the wall. He heard a frantic opening and closing of drawers and what sounded like a safe slamming shut. Reaching the top, he made himself flat against the wall. Peeking around the corner, he saw an open door where he thought the noises had been coming from.

He took a deep breath and slid around the corner. He took two quiet steps, then just before the third, he heard a hammer cock, and he paused. A shot splintered the door frame where Elijah's next step would have been, and he rushed into the room, firing into the corner that Frank Tucker had just dove away from, popping up on the other side of the room. The men now had their guns pointed at each other, Elijah keenly aware he only had one round left.

"Well, that was close on both accounts, Captain," Tucker said.

"It's over, Frank," Elijah said. "We've taken the town back from your men. Who knows how many are even left alive? Two more are dead downstairs." Elijah saw two overstuffed saddlebags lying in front of the safe. "But you don't care about that, do you, Frank? Sure, you lost your town and all your men are dead or in custody, but you'll make off with a good chunk of your fortune and leave them to their fates." He stared at Frank and adjusted his grip on his gun.

"You got me," Tucker said. He gave an exasperated sigh as if he was bored with Elijah's observation. "That's why I always get what I want and come out OK, though. Unlike my pa, unlike you, I'm a survivor who puts myself first."

Elijah bristled. "Killing good people along the way, shirking service to your country, burning an innocent woman's livelihood to the ground, and almost killing her son."

Tucker briefly raised his eyes, then lowered them to Elijah and smiled. "And now I'll get away with it again," he said.

A Lot of People Did

—•—

Elijah felt a hand grab the back of his collar and throw him to the ground at the top of the stairs. Elijah struggled to his feet to find his assailant and Charlie Wade kicked him hard in the side, sending Elijah crashing down the stairs, his revolver clattering away on the bar floor.

"Excellent as always, Charlie," Tucker said. He gathered up the saddlebags and crossed the landing to a back set of stairs. "See to him and meet me out back." He briefly paused near the railing overlooking the bar. "Farewell, Elijah Barber."

Elijah heard Wade's boots pounding down the stairs as he lay on the floor, painfully gasping for breath, blood coming from his nose after it had smashed into the railing. He tried to shake the confusion out of his head and, summoning a will to survive, got to his hands and knees and began fruitlessly scanning the floor for his revolver.

Then he felt the steel of Charlie Wade's revolver in the back of his head.

"Any last words, Barber?"

Elijah said a quick prayer, resigned to his fate. "Is he worth all this to protect, Charlie?"

"Not your concern any longer." Wade cocked the hammer.

Elijah closed his eyes and chose his last thought to be that the quieting of shooting coming from the street meant Moses had won the day.

"Hands in the air!" Marshal Foster's voice boomed from the doorway.

Elijah blew out a deep breath of relief and heard Wade growl in frustration.

He heard the marshal walking toward them. "Drop it now, Wade. You're dead if you don't."

Elijah felt the gun fall away from his head. "I'm dead no matter what, Marshal."

"You never know," Marshal Foster said. He stepped closer. "Just drop the gun."

Elijah still hadn't moved, frozen on his hands and knees. However, he dropped his head and relaxed when he heard the gun clatter to the floor.

Marshal Foster lowered his weapon. "Are you OK, Elij—"

The back door opened suddenly, and Tucker looked directly at Marshal Foster and Wade with his hands in the air. "Oh, for God's sake, Charlie." Tucker fired two quick rounds, one slamming into Marshal Foster's chest and bringing him to the ground.

"No!" Elijah howled. He rose from the ground with a knee into Wade's midsection, grabbed the revolver at his side, and fired two wild shots toward Tucker's backside as he escaped. Seeing Wade writhing on the floor with no weapon nearby, he ran for the door, firing two futile shots at Frank Tucker, who already had his horse moving quickly away from the building and town.

Elijah returned inside and smashed the butt of the revolver across Wade's face as he moved toward Marshal Foster, who had slid himself up against the bottom of the stairs. Elijah heard a rush of activity near the front doorway and looked up to see Moses, George, and Hobbs.

"Guard all the doors!" Elijah shouted.

"What's going on?" asked Moses.

"Did he get away?" Hobbs was reloading his weapons and looking around the bar.

"Is it over out there?" Elijah was getting Marshal Foster's coat off and inspecting the damage.

"Yeah, Elijah," George said. "We won."

"Then just guard the doors."

The three took up posts, saw Elijah tending to Marshal Foster, and realized what was happening.

"Oh Lord," Moses said. "He finally came out during the fight, Eli. When we told him you went for Tucker, he just marched straight through the street toward the saloon and took out two fellers along the way."

Elijah stared wide-eyed at Moses momentarily, then returned his attention to Marshal Foster.

"You with me, Solomon? Stay with me. We'll get you some help."

The marshal looked down at his formerly white shirt, already soaked in red. He looked back up, his face white, and smiled at Elijah. "Can't amputate for that, can you?" He nodded down at the coat Elijah had pulled off him. "Be sure that paperwork gets to the proper authorities," he said softly. "I'd hate any of this to be undocumented . . ." He coughed, blood appearing at the corner of his mouth. "Or for you boys not to get paid."

Elijah forced a smile, a tear in his eye.

"And will you please deliver that letter to my wife?" He reached up, grabbing Elijah and pulling him close. "She knows my shame. Tell her I died doing right for these people, though." He fell back against the stairs, his breathing becoming very shallow.

"You know I will, Marshal."

The marshal closed his eyes and nodded. "Thank you," he whispered. Then he struggled to give a wave of his hand. "For all of it."

He slumped to the side, and Elijah removed the documents from his coat, then laid him flat and covered him.

Standing, Elijah wiped his eyes with his arm and removed his hat, the others following suit. He stuck Wade's revolver in the small of his back, then calmly retrieved his own from the center of the bar floor. He stopped momentarily, Moses, George, and Hobbs all watching him.

Elijah then pulled his slouch hat back on his head, marched across the room to Charlie Wade, snatched him by the coat collar, and began dragging him toward the door, rage in his eyes. "He just saved himself at the expense of others as usual, Charlie. He finally ran out of sacrifices that weren't you, though."

Moses was the first to put his hat back on and quickly follow. "Eli, what are you doing?"

Wade bumped into tables and chairs on the way, and Elijah didn't slow down when he heard Wade grunt from the fall to the boardwalk from the door. Ignoring the pain of his fall, he threw Wade down in the middle of the street and kicked him in the side with his cavalry boots, the man coughing and curling up on the ground. The day's setting sun cast a long shadow in front of Elijah.

"Get up!" Elijah yelled. The remaining posse members and other Rockville citizens were gathering in the street. Many were shouting terrible things at Wade. Others were asking where Tucker had gone to. Some, though, were looking on in horror.

"Get up and face these people." Elijah grabbed him by the hair and pulled him to face the assembling group. He leaned down close to Wade. "I've got one round left. Apparently, I had just enough ammunition to see this day through." He drew the revolver, holding it at his side, and many in the crowd gasped while others encouraged him.

Hobbs spoke up from the side of the street. "These people got their town back, Eli. Folks are gonna get full control of their businesses back, bank and train folks are going to get compensated. Lot of these people have some bounty money coming."

"Eli." Moses was inching toward him, his hands held in front of him. "Remember what Talbot said? We got what it takes to do things to right some wrongs. We done that." He moved toward his brother. "You said yourself, we weren't going to shoot anyone not shooting at us or who had given up." He looked down at Wade. "He ain't fighting you no more, Eli."

Elijah's nostrils flared, and he eyed the crowd. He wiped the blood from his nose and adjusted his grip on the revolver at his side.

Moses cautiously approached Elijah, limping after his tussle inside the blacksmith. Turning his back to the crowd, he spoke in a low voice. "It's not your fault he got away last time, and it ain't this time, either. These people got their town back because of you." Moses looked down at Wade, then back to Elijah, staring at him until their eyes met. "This ain't who you wanna be, brother."

Elijah shook his head and looked down at the ground, then back at Moses. "No, but it's who I am now."

"Nah," Moses replied. "You can be the guy busting down doors, riding fearless into gunfire, risking your life to save my behind and a whole town"—he paused momentarily—"but you ain't this."

The crowd began to part in the middle, and Elijah saw Mary Adams emerge with Johnny, who was leading Bear and Copper. She held a hand to her mouth, apparently understanding the situation.

Johnny did not, however, and called out to Elijah. "We brought your horses back to you, Deputy Barber. My ma says you saved our town, just like you saved me."

Moses turned at the boy's voice and put a hand on Elijah's shoulder. "You hear that, brother?"

Elijah holstered the revolver, then pushed up his hat and rubbed his brow. "A lot of people did, Johnny," he said with a catch in his throat. He looked at George Adams, Clara White, and the brave Rockville and Parke County residents who had fought on this day. Then he turned and looked at his brother, who had a smile on his face. "OK, Mo."

Moses walked away to reunite with Copper, lifting the boy in the air and thanking him. Elijah saw Copper bobbing his head enthusiastically at Moses's attention. *God bless ol' Ben for bringing those animals into our life*, he thought.

The crowd seemed to relax, breathe a sigh of relief, and begin to congratulate themselves. Elijah gently reached under Wade's arm and pulled him up. The man turned and looked Elijah in the eyes.

"He ain't," Wade said.

Elijah raised an eyebrow.

"You asked me if he was worth all this to protect." He turned his head in the direction Tucker had ridden off. "He ain't. I know what I've got comin' to me, but if I'm going down, I might still be able to bring him down with me."

"Alright then," Elijah said. He saw Sheriff Miller and his deputy walking toward them, the deputy holding some shackles. "See him locked up, and don't let anyone near him," Elijah said. "He and I need to chat, and I want him to have a trial."

"You got it, Marshal. He'll be alone in the office cell. We've got the others tied up at the blacksmith."

Elijah hesitated, wondering if the sheriff meant to imply he was now the acting Marshal. He shook it off, however, and handed Wade over to them. The sheriff began leading him away but stopped and turned back to Elijah.

"Your brother," he said.

Elijah was watching the scene unfold but looked back at Sheriff Miller. "What about him?"

"I think he saved as many of ours as he shot of theirs," the sheriff said. "Telling people where to go, droppin' their guys when our folks missed." The sheriff scratched his head. "Don't think I ever saw him crouch or flinch. Never seen anything like it." He shook his head and walked away.

Elijah saw Moses checking on Copper and smiled. *I guess he was right about this being what we're good at.*

AFTER SHAKING HANDS with many of the townspeople, checking on the wounded, and offering his condolences to some kin of the fallen, Elijah found Mary and Johnny and let the boy ride down the street atop Bear.

"You think you could walk him and Copper to the livery and see about them getting rubbed down and fed?"

The boy's eyes lit up, and he looked at his mother.

"Well, of course you can," she said.

Elijah bent down with a grimace and stuck a coin in the boy's shirt pocket while peeking up at Mary, who just shook her head. "Tell them I'll pay for all the hay and oats they want, but you keep that." He looked up at Mary and winked. "Don't tell your mama, though."

The boy smiled and backed away, a look of pride on his face.

She pointed to the livery down the street and saw its owner out front. "Go on," she said.

The two watched the boy lead the horses away for a moment, the livery owner waved to them, and they turned back to each other.

"You're sweet to put on a brave face for him just now," Mary said.

"Wasn't that long ago I would have had to guard every coin I had with my life," Elijah mused. He knew she meant the big picture of the day, the loss of two good men, and the suffering done to save the town.

Mary smiled. "This town will never be able to repay you," she said. Elijah noticed she had the same tired eyes as when he'd met her, but now they had a tinge of hope instead of fear. She reached for his face and turned his head to inspect the injuries. "Are you OK?"

"Ow!" He winced, then laughed.

"Seems you'll be OK physically," she said.

"Mighty sore, but nothing lasting. How about you? Are you and Johnny going to be OK?"

She looked toward her burnt-out store, then back at him. "We will be. Already seems that a lot more folks are willing to be helpful, now that he's gone."

Elijah gestured to the mercantile being built onto the saloon. "There's an office up there with a safe and drawers full of papers. I'm sure one of them talks about who owns the new mercantile. I know buying up cheap businesses that have suddenly become available is a bit of a sore spot in town, but . . ." He trailed off.

She smiled, then he heard her laugh for the first time. He smiled too, but it disappeared when he saw the town's undertaker walking into the saloon.

"Your friend the old sheriff, too?" Mary asked gently.

Elijah looked back to the sheriff's office and nodded slowly. "Had the most meaningful talk I've ever had with someone just before," he said. "Was still alive and shooting when we left him, and I'll choose to remember him that way."

She stepped forward, hugged him, and he let it all go finally, allowing her to embrace him for a full minute. When they separated, he smiled at her.

"He told me to have him buried here," Elijah said. "That there was no use sending him home when his wife and son weren't there." He looked her in the eyes. "Said he wanted to give you all something to remember what happened here."

"We can see to it," she said. "You're leaving soon, then?"

"Shortly, to get after Tucker, I expect. I need to get a trial arranged quickly, though." He looked over to see Moses, Hobbs, George, and Clara talking in front of the sheriff's office. "I'm sure they are waiting for a plan."

She waved at them, and they all waved back, then turned away, embarrassed they'd got caught watching. Elijah and Mary both chuckled.

"Thank you," she said. He began to speak, but she cut him off. "For what you've shown my boy these last couple days."

If he wasn't blushing already, he was after she stood on her toes and kissed his cheek before walking away.

Elijah turned toward the sheriff's office and held a hand up when he saw Moses give him a goofy grin. Elijah smiled too, but both smiles fell away when Elijah reached the sheriff's door and removed his hat.

"You been in yet?" Elijah asked.

"Waiting for you, brother."

THEY WALKED INSIDE the sheriff's office and saw Talbot's body fully covered in the back corner.

"Undertaker said he'd be by shortly, but I knew you'd want to see him," Sheriff Miller said.

"Thank you," Elijah said. "And thank you for coming back."

The sheriff lowered his head.

"He was a big help there at the end," Moses said.

"You did right last night and today, and that's what matters now," Elijah said. "Make sure right gets done by all these people, and take care of this town from now on."

The sheriff shook Elijah's hand and went to the desk to give them some privacy.

Elijah and Moses walked over to Talbot, and Elijah was about to pull back the blanket, then stopped himself. "You OK if we just have our last memory of him be that talk, and him shooting from the doorway?"

"Was hoping you would go that route," Moses said. He cleared his throat. "Seems about right."

Elijah did hope to take something with them to remember him by, but searching his bags found only ammunition, a change of clothes, and some jerky.

"That shouldn't have surprised me, old man," Elijah said with a smile. "We'll leave your revolver with you though." He folded his hands and bowed his head, and Moses joined him. After a moment, he turned for the door.

Reaching for the handle, Elijah stopped and turned. "Deputy Owens."

The young man stood up and walked over to them. "Yessir?"

"How did it happen?"

The young man gulped.

"Go on, then. It's fine," Elijah said.

"He dropped one of them riding by chasing you," the deputy said. "Then he collapsed. I ran over and dragged him inside, shut the door, and moved him against the wall there." The deputy pointed just next to where they stood.

"And he died?" Moses asked.

The young man shook his head. "He started reloading."

Elijah snorted. "Of course he did."

"Said they'd be sending men in for us soon, and told me and the marshal to get ready. I backed away from the door a bit, and the marshal kind of moved into the corner . . ." The deputy trailed off.

"That's alright; he redeemed himself," Elijah said.

"Sure 'nuff, they burst in not a minute later." He pointed to where Talbot had been sitting. "He got one of them almost immediately, and I dropped the second one to come through. A third stormed in, and my cartridge didn't fire. He raised up to fire on me, had me dead to rights, but . . ." His voice caught, and he nodded again at the floor. "Mr. Jones shot him in the head even though he barely looked like he could raise his arm. Fell over just after." He paused as if in reverence. "He saved my life."

Elijah and Moses bowed their heads once again.

"Marshal Foster just sort of stared at him for the longest time, then all the shooting started again. Was like he didn't want to leave him, but when he finally passed, the marshal just marched out into the street."

"Then he came and saved my life," Elijah said. He looked at Moses, who was nodding with his eyes closed. "You done good yesterday and today, deputy. This town is lucky to have you."

Elijah opened the door.

"One more thing."

The brothers turned back.

"When I went over to see if he was gone, he looked up at me and said, 'Tell those damn Barber boys I'm proud of them.'"

Moses patted Elijah on the shoulder and walked out. Elijah looked back to where the old sheriff lay, then walked out and shut the door behind him.

Epilogue

Six weeks later . . . aboard the steamboat Colorado—Missouri River

Frank Tucker walked up the steps to the boat's large salon and could hear the muffled music from within. Opening the door, the banjo and fiddle music poured out, a crowd of people stomping and clapping to the beat. After nearly two weeks of keeping a low profile in his room as a passenger out of St. Louis, he felt secure enough to scratch the itch gnawing at him since he heard the clinking of poker chips a few evenings before.

When he'd found out this trip upriver included a large group of people headed to Montana with a wedding along the way and a handful of executives sailing for Omaha's *Union Pacific* headquarters, it seemed like the trip for him. There had been a great deal of carrying on each night, but this night was the wedding itself, and the celebration was in full swing. The wedding party was the focus, people were drunk, and rich folks wanted to rub elbows with commoners. *A perfect night to win some money at the poker table.*

He'd made his way to St. Louis in a roundabout fashion after completely shaving his face, cutting his hair, and even wearing a pair of spectacles when in a crowd. He had moved from boardinghouse to boardinghouse, waiting for the right boat to take, taking no risks. Now on his way west, effectively leaving the U.S. behind, he breathed easier.

Two poker games were going on this busy night, and he frowned when he saw some of the ship's crew serving as dealers, unlike earlier in the week. He couldn't wholly rig the game, but he still always liked his odds. His Colt pocket revolver and a few twenty-dollar gold pieces were in the pocket of his new suit. Slapping one of the coins on the bar, he asked for a whiskey and some poker chips.

"Good luck, sir," the barman said as he set down the drink and a stack of chips. "Just settle up here when you're all done."

Tucker scratched his clean-shaven face, said thank you, and downed the drink. He sat at one of the tables, waited for a hand to finish, then slid out his ante.

"Welcome, friend," came an excited greeting from one of the players. The man looked like any other wealthy businessman from the East Coast, with too much money and the bravado to head west seeking more.

"Thank you, sir; let's play some cards." He hated small talk with strangers, but everyone was in a festive mood, and he didn't want to draw any negative attention.

The first few hands played out, and Tucker began to understand what he was dealing with while winning a few. The rich man talked too much, which caused him not to pay attention, so Tucker went along.

"I'll wager you aren't with this wedding." Tucker had to practically shout to be heard over the music and the stomping.

The man held a hand to his ear, causing Tucker to repeat himself, then shook his head. "No, no. Headed out west to represent some investors back east. Find out what the gulch towns need."

Sounds like a lot of work when you could steal it from the suckers, Tucker thought. He nodded politely, though. "Well, I'll be sure to let you know what I need when I get there, then." The man smiled back, and the game continued.

An hour or so into the game, Tucker noticed the man regularly looking at a woman seated nearby out of the corner of his eyes. He made a scene of turning and looking at her. "A friend of yours?" he asked. *Now I'll really start to take him if he's worried about a woman.*

The man threw a hand up. "I only wish. Her father is a major backer of the Union Pacific project in Omaha, and she's headed to see him, I hear. So far this trip, she's only paid any attention to men with money." The man made a bet and shook his head. "As if she doesn't have enough already!"

Tucker won another hand and took the occasion of a break in the music to turn around toward the woman, who batted her eyes at him. He stood and walked over to her. "How do you do? My name is Thomas Locke." He had reached a point where lying about his name was no bother and easily done.

She offered her hand and began to speak, but Tucker's attention was caught by a man walking toward the musicians. He now had his back turned, talking to them, but something in the quick side view Tucker saw gave him a familiar feeling. He shook it from his mind and refocused on the woman after missing most of what she said but catching the basics.

"A pleasure indeed, and might I say, you are most lovely." He turned and saw the game at his table breaking up, and the man gave him a wave then walked toward the door with a cigar.

“I hope your game didn’t break up on my account,” the woman said. He hadn’t caught her name but didn’t particularly care. “Will you take the air with me?”

“I will indeed, ma’am.” He smiled. “Let me just settle up those chips.”

He retrieved his sizable stack from the table and walked to the bar, the barman’s eyes bulging. “You made quick work, sir. Cash or house credit?”

“Cash,” Tucker said bluntly.

The man turned away, and the band started up again, the tune sounding very familiar. The woman was at his side now, and he recognized “Kingdom Coming.” He made a face. *How I hate this song,* he thought.

“What’s wrong, Mr. Locke?”

“Oh nothing,” he said. The bartender gave him his winnings, and he returned a coin to impress the woman. “I just knew a man in the war who liked to play it too often.”

He escorted the woman to the door and opened it for her, then guided her down the stairs to the deck. They briefly walked arm in arm, then she stopped at a point on the railing and looked out to the river. The music, stomping, and clapping up above was muffled; the only other sound of the night being the powerful churn of the paddle wheel.

“What a beautiful evening,” she said. “Don’t you think, Mr. Tucker?”

“Why yes it—” He pushed away from the railing. “What did you say?”

Clara White took a couple of steps backward and smiled at him.

“Did you miss it, Frank?”

Tucker spun to face the voice.

"I know you loved this song," Moses Barber said. He wore a Pinkerton badge and had his hand on his holster.

"You had quite the night at the poker table." Tucker turned to another voice and saw the man from the card table emerge, smoking his cigar. "Shame I'm going to return most of it to the boat." He reached into his jacket pocket. "Almost forgot," Matt Hobbs said. He stuck his badge onto his coat.

Tucker narrowed his eyes and bit his lips. A Pinkerton in front of him, Moses Barber to his left, and a woman working with them behind him. *So that means . . .* He turned to his right just as Elijah Barber emerged from the shadows of the moonlit evening, his badge catching the light just right.

"You armed?" Elijah fixed a stare on Tucker.

Now Frank smiled wide at the theatrics. *Such a shame this will be unobserved by an audience*, he thought. "I am, Marshal." He gave a devilish grin. *Unlike you, I'll resign myself to nothing until I have to.*

"Oh, I'm not a marshal anymore, Frank. Just on loan to Mr. Pinkerton to finish some business. Not that I need motivation to finish it." He took a step closer. "Oh, by the way, Charlie Wade used his last words to ask us to tell you hello."

That scoundrel.

"We had some real nice chats with him before and after the trial," Elijah said.

The two eyed each other. The muffled music and churning water were an odd companion to the moment.

He won't shoot me with people just upstairs or the captain watching from the pilothouse . . .

He turned in a circle, taking them all in with his poker assessment. He eyed Moses closely, who tapped the brim of his hat and smiled. "We were gonna head to St. Louis regardless to see the marshal's widow. As much as I was excited to see a big city, we couldn't pass up taking a ride on the Big Muddy after Charlie Wade decided to really narrow down our search." Moses smiled condescendingly. "I just wish you'd poked your head up to play cards sooner. Eli and I were getting awful tired of hiding in our rooms."

Tucker bristled and looked at Hobbs.

"Oh, I was in Rockville, too," he said. "I spent most of my time picking your men off from the roof." Hobbs grinned. "Was fun to do some old-fashioned detective work and figure out what ship you'd end up on. You did a good job keeping a low profile in the city; I'll give you that." Hobbs looked around. "Not really anywhere to hide now, though, is there?"

Tucker bit his lip and turned to the woman.

"We've met," Clara said. "You just don't recognize me in a dress. George Adams says hello as well."

Tucker focused all his energy on not showing how irate he was. He could still find a way out of this. *They all talk a big game, but he told them he'd be the one to do it, and he doesn't have it in him.* He turned to face Elijah again.

"I know what you're thinking, Frank. I told them you were mine." Elijah glared at him.

Tucker ignored the man being in his head. "First the U.S. Marshals, a group of vigilantes, and now the Pinkertons. Delightful. Look how far we've come!" Tucker said just loud enough to be heard. "Oh, and you just did it perfectly. What an ending. Good show! Good show!" He turned and half bowed to them all.

"Let's end it the easy way, Frank," Elijah said. "We'll take you off the boat in Omaha and be done with it. They might even give you a fair trial and all."

"You two could be useful, you know." He looked at both brothers, then spun in a circle. "All of you, really." Tucker clapped his hands close together at chest level. "Got a good line on a gold claim. We could set aside our differences and get rich together. Pity you couldn't collect the bounty then, but there's so much more to be made." He heard Moses snort behind him.

Elijah shook his head, his hand still on his revolver. "We take you off in Omaha. Walking down the plank or in a pine box, Frank. The bounty jumping days are over."

Tucker nodded as if to consider this, then turned his gaze to the moonlit tree line off the starboard side, watching the river pass by, taking the moment in. *I'll be remembered for all this.* Then, deciding to test the man's resolve, he suddenly reached into his coat and withdrew the pocket revolver.

Elijah drew with his right hand, cocking the revolver with his left as he brought it up, and fired into Tucker's chest. He spun the revolver and re-holstered it. The brief crack and echo of the shot were replaced by the noise of the churning water and music again. Tucker faltered backward, gave Elijah a pained grin, shook his head, and fell to the ground.

"Not so formidable when he isn't exploiting folks or taking them by surprise," Hobbs said.

Elijah crossed the distance to where Frank Tucker had fallen. He kicked the pocket revolver away and knelt to check his pockets. He removed a single ace and stood up.

"Wanted to be found with it," Moses said. He hadn't moved from his position leaning on the railing.

Elijah nodded, patting Moses on the shoulder as he walked to the edge and dropped the card below. The ace sat momentarily on top of the water and then was pulled under, caught in the churn of the paddle wheel as the boat continued upstream.

The Barber brothers stood at the bow, Matt and Clara joining them, watching the water and the shoreline slowly crawl by in the bright moonlight as the steamer powered upstream toward Omaha.

"Mr. Pinkerton could sure use a group like you," Hobbs said. "Especially you, Clara. He has a growing number of talented women spies and detectives."

"It's been a pleasure, gentlemen. I was here to ensure this moment then return to Rockville, though."

Hobbs nodded. "And the Barber brothers? Can I talk you into Chicago, or is it back to Danville?"

Elijah looked at Moses, who was staring straight ahead at the river. He put a hand on his brother's shoulder, and Moses smiled. "I think we'll just see what Omaha holds for us. Maybe find our next adventure there," Elijah said.

Thank You

Thank you for reading! If you enjoyed the first installment of the Barber brothers' adventure toward the West, please consider leaving a review on Amazon, or platforms like Goodreads. This is the best way to support the authors you enjoy and help ensure others find this story too! Book two, *The War Remains*, is available now!

I'd also like to thank my editors, Matt Henderson-Ellis and Dave Valencia. After writing 80 percent of this novel, I became stuck tying it to the ending I envisioned. Matt was one of the only freelance editors willing to work with a first-time fiction author and my unfinished manuscript. Were it not for his editorial analysis, developmental edit, and plot suggestions, this work would not exist.

Dave provided a very robust, late-in-the-game copyedit that included generous suggestions for tightening plot points. The story came together over time but would not be the polished product it is were it not for him.

An additional thank-you to the handful of people who were kind enough to read drafts of this story and give me real, honest feedback. Nothing beats a genuine critique from a potential reader!

Finally, a tremendous thank-you to my wife, my number one partner in life. She understands me well enough to know that I need writing in my life but reminds me that it comes after the top priorities of family and my day job. Her support and grounding are something I would fail in life without.

—JBB

About the Author

Jason Baker is a career military officer and celebrated author deeply immersed in the Civil War era. His non-fiction book *Chicago To Appomattox* and his fiction series *The Barber Brothers' Adventures* and *The Vengeance of Reed Caine* are full of meticulous research and classic Western adventure, capturing the tumultuous period of American history.

An Illinois native, Jason resides in Northern Virginia with his wife and two young sons. He is a member of the Western Writers of America, Western Fictioneers, and a Color Bearer Donor to the American Battlefield Trust. Jason dedicates his work to preserving and exploring America's historical landscapes and battlefields. When he's not writing or hiking battlefields, he enjoys following Illinois and Chicago sports teams, waterfowl hunting, and traveling with his family.

Learn more at JasonBakerAuthor.com, or you can also sign up for Jason's Substack newsletter.

www.ingramcontent.com/pod-product-compliance
Lightning Source LLC
LaVergne TN
LVHW010656110826
845149LV00014B/3123